THE COUGH

TANIA DONALD

THE COUGH

RAVENSIN PUBLISHING

Melbourne, Australia.

ISBN: 064821950X

ISBN-13: 978-0648219507

CONTENTS

CHAPTER ONE

It was on a crisp October morning in 1904 that Mr Corliss drew up his cart close by the servants' entrance in the quiet rear courtyard of Wakeley Hall. Mr Corliss looked up at the towering red brick manor house from under the brim of his flat cap and swallowed, feeling a little uneasy.

In the six years since he had moved to Wakeley, he had of course heard of Wakeley Hall and had often seen the tinted picture postcards for sale in the village post office capturing its historic grandeur, but never before had he occasion to visit it – much less to do a job of work there. But owing to the reputation he had earned as a quiet and hard-working carpenter who took a modest pride in the quality of his work – and the fact that Wakeley Hall's elderly resident tradesman had recently been nudged into a somewhat overdue retirement – the summons had at last fallen to Mr Corliss.

In the village of late it had been commented upon frequently, and with some ambivalence, that since the current owner of the Hall, Mr Charles Antony Astley, had brought home his American bride, the former Miss Vivienne Charlton – of the well-known Boston Charltons – "modernisation" seemed to be the order of the day. The introduction of electric lighting had proved a source of considerable concern among the many local people who loved Wakeley Hall, not in spite of but rather

1

because of its charming Queen Anne architecture and colourful history.

The three-storied red-brick structure, with its elegant and symmetrical style, modestly ornamented with quoined corners in grey stone, and bright terracotta bricks framing its neat rows of white-painted high sash-windows, had been an unchanging constant in the fabric of village life since it had replaced the old Wakeley Hall, whose modest Tudor style had been deemed inadequate to the rising standards of the Baronets of Wakeley in 1710. The large round oeil-de-boeuf window set into the centre of the great pediment that crowned "new" Wakeley Hall, had watched over the surrounding countryside like an unblinking eye across the subsequent centuries, impassively observing the changing fortunes of low and high born alike.

Recent rumours that the shrill ringing of the telephone would soon disturb the stately peace of the Hall had only added to the unease with which the new Mrs Astley was regarded, and the vague sense of disquiet that the whispers of change had conjured into the autumn air.

Mr Corliss had little opinion on the matter. As a relative newcomer to the village he had no particular feeling for the Hall save for curiosity. He knew little of its history. He had often thought of visiting the Hall on one of its regular open-to-the-public days in order to see the fine wood-carvings it boasted, but the thought of intruding into the home of a person as rich and prominent as Mr Astley had always intimidated him. What if Mr Astley himself were there? What would be think of the hordes of common strangers nosing around inside his house? If this job were to lead to more work from the Hall's wealthy occupants, then it was all to the good, Mr Corliss thought: provided that he didn't have to have too much to do with Mr or Mrs Astley.

Shyness had always plagued Mr Corliss, and the mere thought of coming under the direct scrutiny of a person of Mr Astley's position and authority was enough to bring blotches of red to the quiet carpenter's neck. He adjusted his neck-cloth, jumped down from the cart and straightened his waistcoat, shaking the thought away. *"It's only wine racks,"* he chided himself. *"A first year apprentice could make such things. Like as not, Mr Astley will never even see them – only his servants."* He moved to the back of the cart, throwing his canvas apron over his arm and pulling out his wooden tool box, as Mr Parker, Mr Astley's genial estate manager, emerged from the Hall's back door to greet him.

"Good morning, Mr Corliss! Oh, that all looks splendid. You had no trouble getting all the timber we talked about, I see?" Mr Parker rubbed his hands together in the chilly morning air: his open face smiling and friendly beneath his neatly combed sandy hair.

"No, sir."

"Good, good. I'll have some of the boys carry it down for you presently. Oh, and your ladders and saw horses and such, of course. Come in, won't you? I'll show you the way."

Mr Parker led Mr Corliss through the busy kitchen and around a back corridor, to where a doorway opened, revealing the staircase down to the cellars.

"I think you'll find this electric lighting a wonderful boon, Mr Corliss. It was dashed dark and gloomy in those old cellars before. I'm sure they'll make your job a sight easier. A marvellous innovation, what?"

"I'm – I'm sure, sir."

On they descended, Mr Corliss' tall and lean frame slightly stooping – as was his habit – as he carried his box: its weight familiar and easy in his strong right arm. At last they reached the bottom of the staircase and Mr Parker fumbled for a moment in the darkness, trying to find the light switch. A quiet cough echoed in the dark void and Mr Parker gave a low "Hmm," clearing his throat in consternation. All at once the light came on and Mr Corliss took a few steps into the cellars, setting down his tool box as he looked around the cavernous space that was punctuated with thick brick pillars supporting the many groined arches of the vaulted ceiling above. At the far end of the chamber he saw an open archway that led into further darkness beyond.

Mr Corliss' eyes scanned the dusty wooden wine-racks that lined the walls and the innumerable bottles they held.

"I should explain, Mr Corliss. This part of the cellar has long been in use for storing wine and liquors, as you may see, but Mr Astley has decided to expand his collection further, into the cellar beyond: Mrs Astley wishes to do a great deal more entertaining at the Hall, you see. The entranceway to the second cellar had been stopped up with a great stack of old boxes and old furniture – piled quite up to the ceiling! I think the family had entirely forgotten there was anything behind it."

"I see."

"So come through, won't you, and I'll explain."

Mr Parker strode on ahead, another low cough resounding through the arches as they walked. Mr Parker looked over his shoulder at Mr Corliss with a thin smile in his eyes as they reached the open archway and felt blindly again for the light switch in darkness of the next cellar. Mr Parker gave a nervous laugh before succeeding in switching on the light with a satisfied "Ah." The second cellar appeared identical to the first, save for its arched red brick walls being empty of shelves. A stubborn smell of mildew and must hung in the air, which the recent influx of fresh air and the new electric lighting had so far failed to dispel.

"I do apologise for the close atmosphere in here, Mr Corliss. I'm sure that with your coming and going, and the boys as well, it will get the air moving around down here and freshen things up a bit."

Mr Parker drew a large folded paper from his pocket and pulled it open, moving more directly under one of the bare hanging light globes and gesturing with his head for Corliss to come nearer.

"Do you see, Mr Corliss? It is just as I explained to you when I came to your workshop the other week. Mr Astley wishes the racks to line both of these long walls that extend the length of the cellar – just as in the previous room. I'm sure you will find our measurements and estimates were correct: Mr Astley does us like to be very thorough with all of these projects of his. He supervised the drawing up of these plans himself."

Mr Corliss nodded. It struck him then how very cold the cellar was, and he pulled his neck-cloth up higher, urging himself to remember to wear something warmer tomorrow.

"Very good, sir," Mr Corliss affirmed quietly, nervous of the way that the echoing cellar seemed to make his voice sound louder. "It all seems straightforward enough," he murmured.

"Good, good." Mr Parker gave the plans to Corliss and clapped his hands together, rubbing them against the chill in the air. "Well, I shall leave you to it, Mr Corliss. The boys will soon be along with your supplies, and they can help you in any way you might require – ah, when they are free from their other duties around the estate and the farm, that is. Likewise, if you wish to speak to me about anything, you have only to ask one of the men to fetch me, or if you go back up the stairs to the kitchen, Mrs Gardiner or one of the other staff will know how to find me. Oh, and I've told Mrs Gardiner to expect you for your tea breaks and your dinner. You'll find she's a splendid cook. Right, well … " Mr Parker smiled warmly.

"Thank you, sir. I'll make a start then."

Mr Parker nodded pleasantly and turned on his heel, his brisk footsteps echoing after him. Mr Corliss felt relieved to be left alone and looked around the empty space, moving to inspect one of the walls. The old red bricks were of the highest quality and he patted the wall with his broad left hand: the missing tip of his ring finger still catching his eye, even after all these years. The wall was very cold and reassuringly solid. His nose wrinkled slightly at the prospect of all the holes he would have to drill and hoped his trusty bit and brace was up to the task of boring into such monumental masonry. He gave an involuntary shiver. "*Never mind the cold, William,*" he chided himself, "*all this work will get you warm soon enough.*"

The first week's work had progressed well. Mr Corliss soon worked out the times when the young men from the Hall's farm were free to help him, and planned his day according to the work he could do unaided and the work for which a second or even a third pair of hands was helpful. And if the boys happened to be free unexpectedly, he had set the more capable ones to work in sawing the milled timber into the correct lengths, before he finishing dressing the wood himself. Neat, new wine racks now lined the walls between the pillars of four of the indented archways, and Mr Parker seemed very pleased with the progress that had been made. Mr Corliss was also pleased, and rather relieved that Mr Astley himself had not, thus far, come to inspect the works.

The masonry, however, had proved to be just as hard and unyielding as Mr Corliss has suspected and he had had to purchase extra drill bits against the blunting effect of the bricks. He had found that the best thing was to place the head of the brace against his chest, rather than in his hand, so that the full weight of his body could be brought to bear upon the drill as it bit into the bricks. And so it was that he positioned himself once again, early on the following Monday morning, in the silence and stillness of the chilly cellar.

Having marked his position on a new section of wall precisely with the flat carpenter's pencil that he had always at the ready, he carefully situated the pointed tip of the drill bit, held the head of the brace to his chest and leaned the full weight of his considerable height and muscle forward as he

began to turn the smooth wooden handle of the drill. He gasped sharply –
startled to feel something yielding under the drill and unable to stop himself
from falling forward as with a terrible scraping and clinking the brickwork
caved in under his weight. Mr Corliss fell onto his hands and knees, his
brace and bit caught between toppling bricks as a gust of powdery dust and
foul smelling air billowed out from the broken wall to engulf him.

Mr Corliss cried out in pain as the sharp edges of the bricks struck into
his palms and the jagged heft of another brick struck his wrist. He sucked in
a breath of air at the hurt and squeezed tight his eyelids against the foul dust
and grit that swirled into his eyes. He began to cough as the dusty cloud
filled his lungs: his nostrils flaring with disgust. The smell was something
quite terrible. It was a mustiness he could taste on his tongue, gritted with
fine particulate matter that instantly irritated his eyeballs, nostrils and
airways: foul with the odour of long decay and old damp air that had been
too long sealed up in darkness. With a panicked jerk of his arms he
extricated himself from the bricks and crawled backwards, his eyes still
screwed tightly shut against the swirling grit and dust. His back butted up
against the woodpile in the middle of the room and he sat down roughly on
the floor, shaking his head and trying to clear his throat. He coughed and
spluttered again, spitting to try to remove the fetid and unwholesome taste
from his mouth: wiping his hands against his dirty canvas apron before
fishing blindly for the handkerchief he always kept in his trouser pocket.

"Oh, my lord," he coughed and spluttered, wiping roughly at his
streaming eyes to get the dust and grit away. He blinked open his eyes,
anxious to examine his hands where the pain throbbed fiercely. Sure
enough there were some grazes and a few cuts that now bled starkly red
against the dirty grey of his dust-covered skin.

"Oh dear." He frowned at his hands and wound the handkerchief
around his left hand where the worst cuts were. He winced at the thought

of having to summon Mr Parker and what a hindrance this mishap might cause to his work. The last thing he wanted was Mr Astley coming down to see what had happened and thinking that he had accidentally destroyed a portion of the wall through poor workmanship. Mr Corliss coughed again, waving his throbbing hands to try to clear the sickly charnel-house stench that still swirled in the dusty air and befouled his mouth and nose. He looked up to the broken wall and fell sharply back against the woodpile with a shrill scream that echoed horribly through the vaulted space.

He blinked again more furiously and leaned forward, crouching on his knees as he peered into the dusty wall cavity behind the pile of bricks, squinting – feeling his blood run to ice as shock forced the air from his lungs with a shudder. Low down in the wall, peeking out over the jagged bricks that still remained in place he saw hands: two skeletally slender hands covering the top of a desiccated face. Below the hands there was a gaping mouth, frozen in a silent and eternal scream. He was scarcely breathing as he rose to his feet, stifling his coughs with his bound hand as he gingerly drew closer.

"Surely it's some sort of statue," he thought. *"It can't be … can't be … "*

His eyes focused on a rope that bound the wrists: the rope now grown loose as the wrists were shrivelled to bone thinness and covered in skin that looked for all the world like dry and yellowed parchment. He saw hair: remnants of hair that clung to a papery scalp. It was long dusty red hair, and had the suggestion of a curl in the strands that still remained. He took a step closer and peered down behind the bricks, seeing bony knees hunched up under the screaming chin and the remnants of an antique dress: a filthy pale blue dress thick with grey dust.

"No … no!" he cried in a childlike voice that seemed not his own and whose terrible sound only escalated the wild pounding in his chest. Mr Corliss found himself running out of the cellar: that same strange involuntary voice in him crying out in panic: "Mr Parker! Mr Parker! Mr Parker! … "

CHAPTER TWO

Mr Corliss stood silently in a corner of the cellar by the open archway, a blanket around his shoulders as he sipped absently on the mug of hot tea that had been pressed into his hands – by whom, he could not presently recall. He concentrated his thoughts on keeping his bandaged hands from shaking and trying to mask the deep agitation that still urged him, at every second, to run from the dim cellar back up to the daylight and far away from the Hall. His mind churned with an anguish he could not formulate into thought – thoughts too distressing to allow into his consciousness. He took some comfort in the fact that all of the people now so noisily occupying the cellar with him – the two police officers, a Mr Chandler from the British Archaeological Association, Mr Parker with a few of his men from the farm, and the formidable Mr Astley – were so morbidly enthralled with what had been revealed behind the wall, that none of them were paying him the slightest attention. No-one registered his profound distress. "*It's all right*," Mr Corliss thought to himself, "*it will be all right. Just take yourself in hand.*"

"Well, I can reassure you of one thing, Mr Astley," Mr Chandler pronounced, wiping the dust from his spectacles before replacing them on his ruddy and perspiring face. "As I'm sure you will have surmised, the

unfortunate young lady has lain here for some considerable length of time –
this is no recent crime, if crime it is. Of course I can't move anything until
the county coroner arrives, but from what I can see of her costume, the
textiles, the twine around her wrists and so forth, I would estimate
somewhere in the mid eighteenth century. I would guess the 1740s to 50s?"

"Yes, yes," the police inspector interjected confidently to Mr Chandler
with furious nodding. "That is just what I was saying to my constable here
before you arrived, wasn't I, Constable Clarke? Eighteenth century indeed,
Mr Astley."

Mr Chandler shot the inspector a sideways glance. "Naturally, Mr Astley
we can't be certain until a more detailed examination has taken place, but I
am fairly sure that we will be able to date these remains to the time of the
former Baronetcy of Wakeley: I have rather a strong suspicion they might
be from the time of Sir Benjamin Stockard himself, the last Baronet."

Mr Corliss was startled by the sudden scent of perfume and shrank back
further into the corner as Mrs Astley swept silently into the cellar. Mr
Corliss gave a little shiver and his eyes winced in pain as the frilled skirts of
her voluminous mauve day dress glided over the dirty floor. She clutched at
the fur wrap that was fastened around her slender shoulders and Mr Corliss
noted that its pale silvery blonde colour was almost the exact same shade as
the lustrous hair that crowned her head in such an impossibly artful
arrangement.

"Aha, back in the good old days when the landed gentry could do
whatever they pleased, eh?" Mr Astley joked loudly, heedless of the strident
volume of his voice in the echoing chamber. "Why, there are one or two
people I should very much like to brick up inside a wall myself if only one
could still get away with such things, eh, Inspector!"

"Does anybody know who she was?" Mrs Astley's unexpected and
feminine voice, with its startlingly foreign accent, silenced the men's polite

laughter.

"Oh, I didn't see you there, my dear. I shouldn't come too near, Vivienne," Mr Astley warned gently. "It's … well, rather grim, I'm afraid. But it all happened long in the past, I'm assured, so it's nothing we need be too bothered about."

"Mrs Astley does raise rather an interesting question though, sir," Mr Chandler mused, politely inclining his bald head in Mrs Astley's direction. "I'm sure you noticed the red hair on the young woman – a remarkably vivid shade of red even now. It's not a colour we see very often around here. If we *can* date the remains to the Baronetcy of Sir Benjamin, that detail of the hair colour is rather suggestive, don't you think?"

Mr Astley gave a dismissive laugh. "Pshaw! Surely no-one takes any of those silly old folk tales seriously nowadays, Chandler?"

"Well, sir, very often we do find there is a grain of truth in these local legends. I would not be too quick to dismiss the possibility – as fanciful as it might at first seem."

Mrs Astley shivered and gathered her wrap more tightly around her shoulders, taking a step closer and craning her neck to see the spectacle that Chandler and the policemen were trying to block from her view. "What local legend is that?" she asked curiously.

"The one about, ah, poor old Sir Benjamin, my dear. You remember, you read it out to me from that book about the history of Wakeley Hall that you found in our library – last winter wasn't it? I'm sure you recall." Mr Astley folded his arms, and twitched his dark moustache: his feet becoming restless in growing boredom.

"Oh yes, of course." Mrs Astley swept a stray strand of hair from her face. "Sir Benjamin, the last Baronet of Wakeley. Oh that was a terribly sad story. You can't mean, Mr … ?"

"Chandler, madam."

"Mr Chandler, you're not suggesting that this could be the red-headed woman who was supposed to have killed them all? Why, in the book it said that Sir Benjamin had had her sent away to prison before he died – how *could* it be her?"

Mr Chandler winced, minding his words. "Well, Mrs Astley, as Mr Astley pointed out, the landed gentry in those days often did mete out a kind of rough justice – in a place like this, there was very often no-one else to deal with local matters of law and order. And let us not forget that they lived in superstitious times: a person who was seen as a harbinger of disease might easily have been regarded by some as a witch or an agent of some supernatural evil. It has been suggested that in centuries past, the origins of the vampire legends might have come from simple people's demonising of tuberculosis victims and blaming them for the inevitable spread of the disease – even going so far as staking them in their graves to try to halt the spread of the 'evil'." Mr Parker gestured to the broken wall behind him. "If she was indeed the source of the tuberculosis, perhaps this was an attempt to halt the contagion by containing the carrier of the disease. In desperate and fearful times, people will try extreme measures … I shouldn't wonder that Sir Benjamin would conceal such an act from posterity with a false story about prison or transportation or the like. I expect he was only trying to protect the people of Wakeley, even if it was by some terrible act of superstition."

"It said in the book, Mr Chandler, that the young woman deliberately infected the Stockard household with tuberculosis because she was madly in love with Sir Benjamin and he refused her. She was a maid, lowly born, and he was already married to Lady Stockard. Isn't that how the story goes? Wasn't she supposed to have been disordered in her mind?"

"I believe that she was said to have been a dairy-maid from Wakeley Hall farm, Mrs Astley, as I recall. And it was alleged by another milk maid that the young woman had been secretly coughing and spitting her disease into the milk and cream that was sent up to Sir Benjamin and his wife every day from the farm. Sadly, when she was found out it was all too late for the family and household. In these enlightened times I suppose we would say she was quite insane, hysterical or something like that … "

Mr Astley gave an exasperated sigh and scuffed his feet on the dirty brick floor. "Mr Chandler, if you don't mind, I hardly think this a fit subject to discuss in front of my wife. Indeed, my dear, I find the whole matter quite distasteful."

Mr Chandler bowed his shiny head as the police inspector looked on with quiet satisfaction. "I do apologise, Mr Astley … madam."

The police inspector cleared his throat and raised his nose in the air over Mr Chandler's shiny head. "Well, whatever the truth was, it's all academic now, wouldn't you say, Mr Chandler? You can have all the colourful theories you like, but I don't see how anyone can prove who was who or who did what at this late stage, short of there being some sort of a signed confession in there with her."

"Quite right, Inspector." Mr Astley nodded and put his fists on his hips, drawing himself up to his full height. "What does it really matter now at any rate? Yes, it's very unfortunate, but it's all in the past. Let the coroner come and deal with it and we can get on with more important things. Have you ordered that new farm machinery we talked about yet, Parker?"

Mrs Astley silently raised an eyebrow and turned around, starting at the sight of Mr Corliss' ashen face in the gloom of the dark corner where he was still cowering. She clutched her throat. Mr Corliss gave an embarrassed cough, nodding his head briskly towards Mrs Astley, and averting his eyes as Mr Astley and the others noticed him. He swallowed hard against the raspiness he felt in his throat.

Mrs Astley took a step forward, her long and delicate face pained with concern. "Is this the poor man who … ?"

Mr Parker stepped forward. "Yes, Mrs Astley, this is Mr Corliss who made the discovery."

"What a terrible shock for you, Mr Corliss. Charles, oughtn't we to send Mr Corliss home for the day? He's as white as a sheet."

Mr Astley strode over to Mr Corliss' corner and peered at him, smoothing down his dark and neatly trimmed moustaches. "You're alright, aren't you … er, Corliss? I'm sure you'll be fine once you've had your tea and you can get back to work."

Mr Corliss tried to slow his breathing, aware of the heat rising in his neck and face and wishing only to escape Mr Astley's pitiless scrutiny. "F– fine, thank you, sir." Mr Corliss gave an involuntary cough, and felt his face redden all the more as he tried to stifle the irritation at the back of his throat. "Just the dust, you see," he rasped quietly, trying to suppress the unbearable tickling sensation.

"Good man. Splendid." Mr Astley turned on his heel and left the cellar, his wife following close behind.

Mr Corliss forced a smile as Mr Parker approached him and put his hand on Corliss' shoulder. "You don't look well, Mr Corliss, why don't you go home for the afternoon. The Inspector has your statement about what happened. I can't see that you'll be able to do anything more today what with everyone milling around in here and the coroner coming and … everything else that must be done."

"That's good of you, sir. If you're sure it's all right?"

"Oh yes, quite sure. Go and get some fresh air." Mr Parker smiled gently.

Mr Corliss drained the last of the tea from his cup and remembered that he had better pack up his tools into his toolbox, lest they be left in the way of the coroner and everyone else. As he crouched down to pack his things away, he noticed Mr Parker's men, now that Mr Astley had gone, edging forward to get a better look at the body in the wall cavity. Two of the younger ones seemed to be silently urging their older friend to say something to Mr Chandler, the archaeologist.

"Mr Chandler?" the braver youth began, "did you know that the ghost of Waverley Hall is supposed to be tied up with old Sir Benjamin and this business with the red-headed girl?"

"I had heard local stories to that effect, yes," Mr Chandler replied, wearily.

"It's Lady Stockard's coughing that's heard in the house sometimes, so they say," one of the other young men added.

The Inspector rolled his eyes and walked off to talk to Mr Parker who was standing near the distant entrance of the first cellar, waiting for the coroner by the foot of the stairs.

"Have you seen this alleged ghost then, young man?" Mr Chandler asked, his eyebrows raised sceptically over his spectacles.

"Nay, nobody's seen it – but we've all heard it, like." The young man's companions all nodded earnestly. "Like a lady coughing something terrible – but sort of far away, like she's always in another room, but you can never find her. They say that she was infected while with child and that the child was born infected with the consumption too and she watched it die, before she herself was taken. And poor old Sir Benjamin, he saw it all and was the last one to die, some months later, God rest his soul."

"And what does Mr Astley have to say about these ghost stories?"

"Oh no, he don't believe in such things. He just says that it makes a good story to tell when the house is open to visitors. But you ask anyone who works here. My mother has worked at the Hall since she were only young and she'll tell you the same. Heard it often, she has."

"It's a colourful story, I'll give you that, young man, but I would imagine that in a drafty old house like this, with as many staff as work here, the odds of hearing a real person coughing in a distant room are fairly high, at any time of the day or night. Now I realise that no old country house is complete without some sort of ghost story, but I'm afraid that this business strikes me as simply overactive imaginations."

The young men fell silent and exchanged sheepish glances. Mr Chandler felt bad for embarrassing them with his unromantic realism and softened a little.

"There's no doubting the business with the last Baronet was a very unfortunate thing," Mr Chandler reasoned, taking out his handkerchief and wiping his hands. "You've all seen the Stockard family crypt in the church, I'm sure. All of them dead within two years – as well as many of their household who are buried out in the churchyard – and of course the poor infant who was the last heir to the Wakeley Baronetcy: the end of that noble line. Such a calamity is bound to leave its mark in the minds of a community, and to haunt the memory and the imagination. Perhaps that is all that we can say of such things with any certainty."

Mr Corliss found that he had little appetite for the meal of egg and sausages he had cooked himself for dinner. He was sitting in his well-worn armchair by the fire in his snug little parlour. The gramophone record he had put on to try to distract himself was making a rasping, rhythmic scrape as the needle spiralled endlessly around the spindle. The copy of H G Wells' *Kipps* that he had been attempting to read lay open on the arm of the chair. Once again he realised that he was staring, frowning, into the coals of the fire: his thoughts circling back to the day's events.

He had tried to tell himself that it was all right, that it had all happened so long ago, but the look on the poor young woman's face – that screaming mouth, the contorted and bound hands – had etched its horror into his mind like a burning afterimage from staring too long at the sun.

He had taken a bath to wash the dust and grit away, but still felt somehow soiled. He swallowed another sip of his tea that had gone cold, and he winced. His throat felt irritated and sore. The room felt unusually chilly, even though he was sitting close by the fireplace. He wondered if he was catching a cold, or whether the terrible dust and all his screams had perhaps inflamed his throat. It was the sound that he had made that bothered him now most of all. He had not screamed like that since he was a boy. He had gathered a woollen rug around his shoulders, but he still felt chilled to the marrow.

"Best go to bed, William, and forget all about it," he said to himself gently, his eyebrow raising at the suggestion of hoarseness in his voice. He gave a little cough and cleared his throat.

Mr Corliss passed a restless night, his long limbs twitching and lashing beneath the covers of his single bed. A sheen of perspiration glistened on his long face: his brown eyes searching frantically behind closed lids and his breaths ragged. His short brown hair clung damply to his forehead. Into his nebulous dreams there intruded a sound that woke him with a start: a cough. Mr Corliss's head twisted to the side.

"Who's there?" he rasped, half-asleep, before the sting in his throat brought him more fully to his senses. He felt an itchy spasm in the back of his throat and began to cough, sitting up in his bed, his eyes closed in the darkness, until the moment passed. He cleared his throat and made a little groan as he rubbed at his damp face. He shivered slightly as the night air chilled the perspiration on his skin and pyjamas. *"Must be coming down with something,"* he thought as he swallowed again and lowered his head back onto the pillow. It was still so dark outside. He tried to remember the dream that had troubled him so deeply only a few moments before, but it had escaped him, leaving behind nothing but a feeling of deep unease. Had it been something to do with his mother? His face twitched and he turned to face the other way. *"Go back to sleep, William."*

"Good morning, Mr Corliss!" Mr Parker smiled as Mr Corliss pulled up his cart and jumped down onto the gravel.

"Morning, sir." Mr Corliss cleared his throat and gave Mr Parker a half-smile from under his cap.

"Well, I just wanted to reassure you, Mr Corliss, that everything is fine. It's all been … cleared up down there, so there's nothing more to worry about. The men and I have also made an inspection of the rest of the brickwork in that cellar and all seems quite as it should be. The section in question appears to have been the only one that … had been tampered with in the past. Mr Astley has authorised me to engage Mr Langdale to come and repair that portion of the wall – are you acquainted with Mr Langdale at all?"

"Aye, sir. I am," Mr Corliss coughed.

"Ah, splendid." Mr Parker eyed Mr Corliss' face with slight concern. "Ah, well, Mr Langdale is currently occupied, but he will come just as soon as he is finished his present job, so I would suggest you just leave that section of the wall until last, or until later at any rate. I say, are you feeling all right, Mr Corliss?"

"Fine. Fine, sir. Just a bit of a sore throat, that's all."

"Oh, what rotten luck. Well I shall ask Mrs Gardiner to make you some of her honey and lemon tea – marvellous stuff."

"Thank you, sir. Right good of you."

Mr Parker clapped his hands together and rubbed them on the sleeves of his tweed jacket, his breath frosting in the early morning air. "Well then, I must go and see what's happening up in the dairy: some problem with this morning's milk having soured somehow, I am told. A dashed nuisance.

Perhaps I shall see you again this afternoon and make sure you have everything you need." Mr Parker smiled kindly and patted Mr Corliss on the shoulder as he strode off to fetch his horse from the stables. A park and small hill divided the extensive grounds surrounding Wakeley Hall from the farmland and farm buildings some distance behind it and Mr Parker found it more efficient to ride around the large estate than to walk.

Mr Corliss kept his head down as he walked through the kitchen, muttering "Morning," and taking off his cap as he carried his toolbox around to the stairway. He could sense morbid interest in the way the cook and kitchen maids stared at him now and he did not wish to be drawn on the subject of yesterday's events any further. He only wanted to forget it.

The staff had all been friendly enough over the previous week, but there was something in Mrs Gardiner's attention to him on the previous occasions that he had felt brave enough to venture up for a cup of tea that had made him feel somehow uncomfortable. He winced to recall that it had been she who had first seen him in all his distress when he had burst into the kitchen from the cellar yesterday; she who had washed and bandaged his bleeding hands and given him tea so kindly while he had tried to contain his anguish and wished only to be left alone. He didn't want to seem rude, but he had decided to say that he preferred to take his cup back down to the cellar during his tea break and drink it there, as he had so much work to do. And if he *had* accepted her repeated invitation to take his tea and his dinner in the kitchen by the huge fire, how would it have looked if Mr Astley had happened by?

"*Better to keep to yourself,*" he thought, pausing on the staircase to wipe the sheen from his forehead. It struck him then that he did not feel at all well. Even descending the staircase seemed a strain. "*Never mind, there's work that must be done. You might as well feel poorly at work and get paid for it than lie about at home.*"

Mr Corliss stood and stared at the hole on the wall from a distance, where the bricks had fallen in. It gaped in a way that struck him as not just ugly but unwholesome, like someone's broken tooth that kept catching your eye as they spoke, no matter how much you told yourself not to stare at it. The smell of rot still hung uneasily in the air from yesterday. Mr Corliss decided it would be best to start on the other wall today: it made no real difference and at least he would not have to keep looking at the hole if it was behind him.

His work proceeded well, if perhaps not quite at his usual pace. Mr Corliss noticed that his energy was a little diminished, and as the day wore on his work was increasingly interrupted by his coughing. At first it was mainly the impulse to clear his throat all the time and the odd cough, but something about the coldness of the air in the cellar seemed to irritate the back of his throat and his airways and the coughing grew, both in strength and frequency. It grew loud enough to echo disturbingly in the vaulted cellar: loud enough that he worried it would draw undue attention to him from the kitchen above or from Mr Parker, should he hear it. But what troubled him more was the suggestion of a smell. He would cough three or four times and at the very end of the cough there seemed to be a barely perceptible unpleasant odour, never enough to satisfy him one way or another that it was coming from inside him though. *"The air is bad down here,"* he reasoned, *"I smell it as I breathe in, so why would I not smell it as I cough it out too?"* It smelt the same as the foul must in the cellar: a smell of damp and rot.

With no-one to help him, as one of the farm boys had stopped by briefly to say that they were all very busy on Mr Parker's instructions, cleaning and scrubbing out all the dairy equipment, Mr Corliss found himself weary and desirous to go home a little earlier than usual. He had done all that he could for the day and wished only for a hot bath and an early night. He turned around to start packing up his toolbox and was jolted by the sight of the broken wall panel that his strenuous labour, and his preoccupation with his sore throat, had successfully put from his mind.

"It's just a hole in a wall," he thought calmly, thinking himself foolish for the unease he had felt in the morning. He walked around the low stacks of milled timber in the centre of the large room and approached the cavity, suppressing another cough. *"It's really no different from any of the burial crypts in the church with all their old remains, and you never felt funny about those when you were doing all those repairs in the church."* He moved closer to the dark space and peered over the jagged edge of the hole. *"You see, it's quite empty now."* He leaned further and peered a little closer as something caught his eye. Without thinking he reached down and picked up the little dusty silver object that glinted dully in the depths of the shadow inside the broken wall. Mr Corliss gave a slight gasp as the small metal hairpin between his fingers revealed something trailing from it: a long and curling tress of bright red hair. He turned the pin in the light, his eyes widening at the small decorative metal bee that ornamented the pin. He lightly touched the long red hair and absently coiled it around his finger, as the curls seemed so easily inclined to do.

Mr Corliss' head turned sharply at the noise from the direction of the stairway and he began to cough once more, unthinkingly dropping the coil of hair and the pin into the pocket of his apron as the footsteps on the stairs grew louder, and Mrs Gardiner's friendly voice called out.

"I'm sorry to disturb you, Mr Corliss. Only I heard all your coughing, and I thought you might like some of my special tea."

Mr Corliss did his best to smother his coughs, feeling his cheeks colouring with the effort.

"I was just saying to Margaret that the air down here is dreadful and no wonder poor Mr Corliss is coughing like that." She held out the cup, which

Mr Corliss accepted with the hand that was not covering his mouth.

"Ta very much, Mrs Gardiner, that's right good of you," he murmured.

"It's nowt, Mr Corliss." She leaned in closer, lowering her voice. "I'm surprised they didn't just brick up the whole cellar after what you found here yesterday. Making you come back and keep working here after that ... why it's dreadful, it's just dreadful. Oh and this terrible smell hanging in the air – it can't be healthy. Well, it's not for me to say what I really think, but Mr Astley's father would never have been so heartless to his workers. He was a very considerate man, a kind man, and young Mr Astley isn't a patch on the old gentleman if you want to know the truth."

Mr Corliss nodded, in between hasty sips of the honey and lemon flavoured tea, which he would very much have enjoyed in other circumstances. But the scorching heat of the tea, combined with his slight fever, and Mrs Gardiner standing so close to him, all alone in the echoing cellar, was making his head swim.

"You do not look well, Mr Corliss. Are you feeling all right?"

"I'll be fine, thank you." Mr Corliss drained the cup as quickly as he could, in spite of the overwhelming heat of the drink, and held it out towards the concerned cook. "I think I ought to be off home now and get some rest."

"Have you anyone to look after you, Mr Corliss?"

"Nay, I'll be quite all right. It's just a cold or summat." Mr Corliss forced a smile and kept is head down as he hastened to collect his toolbox.

"Would you like me to prepare you a mustard plaster you can apply when you get home? It's no trouble."

Mr Corliss made towards the staircase at the end of the cellar. "Thank you but you needn't trouble yourself, missus. I'll be fine. Thank you." He looked back to see Mrs Gardiner standing before the hole in the wall, his empty cup clasped in her hands.

"'Night," he called over his shoulder, trying to sound cheerful.

"Goodnight, Mr Corliss," the cook's concerned voice echoed after him up the stairs.

It was just before Mr Corliss was about to prepare for bed that night that he remembered the lock of hair and hairpin he had left in his apron pocket: his apron that was still in his cart out in the stable. He hadn't meant to take the lock and pin, but now that he had them he wondered what he ought to do with them. Putting them back where he had found them felt wrong somehow. He warmed himself before the fire, after his quick jog out to the stable to retrieve the lock of hair from the apron in his cart. The cold night air had aggravated his lungs and he had coughed quite badly until he got back to the warmth of his hearth.

He coiled the long tress as neatly as he could and secured it with the pin. For a second he thought of throwing it into the fire but that also seemed wrong. For something so old, the hairpin looked very fine and appeared to be made of silver. The little bee decoration was small but appeared very well made. He wondered how a young dairymaid could ever have afforded such a fancy trinket. The coughing started up again and it was beginning to give him a headache, so he resolved to put the pin and coil of hair away somewhere safe until he could think of what should be done with them.

From the very back of the top shelf of the hall cupboard where he kept the few dusty family mementos he had, Mr Corliss drew out a little wooden musical jewellery box and unlocked it. He tucked the coiled tress into the worn red velvet compartment inside it – alongside his mother's wedding ring, her bent hatpin, and his grandfather's small plain pocket watch and tie pin and grandmother's jet mourning brooch – before quickly locking it up again and tucking it back in its corner, behind some old blankets.

He looked on another shelf and found a box of old medicines, rifling through the assortment of clinking brown glass bottles and disintegrating cardboard boxes and packets, until he lighted upon a dusty bottle of "Pelikan Lung Balsam." The bottle was thick with dust and the peeling label faded. Mr Corliss strained to recall when he might have bought it but could not remember and wondered if this was not another of the various bits of ephemera he had inherited from his grandparents. But as the coughing showed no signs of easing and he wished to get a good sleep, he carried the bottle to the kitchen, straining the unscrew the white metal cap that felt glued on with the sticky residue of the syrup. Pausing for another fit of coughing, he picked up a spoon that was drying on the side of the sink, and took a spoonful of the dense black liquid.

The taste was bitter and herbaceous, but it did feel soothing to his sore throat, and after a few minutes, which he spent changing into his pyjamas and tending to the little coal fire in his room, he felt that the old cough syrup had indeed afforded him some relief. "*A good night's sleep will do you the world of good.*"

Sleep came quickly and Mr Corliss enjoyed several hours of rest, and some pleasant if unusually vivid dreams, before his nocturnal visions took on a less favourable aspect. Somehow, the dark corridor of his childhood home led him into the cellars of Wakeley Hall. He realised as he stood in the second cellar, that a third cellar he had not noticed before extended back into the darkness at the end of the second. Very dimly, in the distance, he thought a low candle flickered even beyond this extra cellar that he had just discovered. How far did the cellars extend back? He strained his eyes against the distant darkness of those unknown vaulted chambers at some shadow he thought he perceived passing before that tiny candle's light, but he could not make it out. Once he had completed his task he could go and look. He had to put back what he had taken and then he could go. Mr Corliss reached into his pocket for the hairpin and its coil of red hair. But instead of the neatly rolled tress he had expected to feel, his fingers tangled in a coarse snarl of dry strands of hair in matted disarray.

He pulled it out of his pocket, or tried to, wishing to make it neat again before putting it back. But the mess of hair was knotted and entwined around his fingers, and as much as he pulled it from his pocket, still more came as he pulled at it and he wondered, with rising alarm, how he could free himself from the hair without breaking it, as he did not wish to damage it.

He had intended only to throw the lock of hair and the pin back into the wall cavity, then continue along through the other cellars, but somehow the long red hair would not allow it. Breathing faster, he nervously stepped nearer the jagged wall cavity, pulling at the tangles of hair that had insinuated themselves around his fingers, tightening and biting into his skin like fine wires. He tried to cast the hair into the void but it stuck to him, entwining tighter around his fingers the more he tried to pull it away, and even as he managed to cast some long strands into the black wall cavity, the strands remained connected to him and began somehow to pull at him from the void. He dragged his heels on the dirty floor stones as the hair drew him in more forcefully, pulling his head in closer to the jagged bricks and that terrible blackness with its rising swirls of pungent and gritty dust.

He scraped his hands over the sharp edges of the bricks, trying to snag the tangles of hair there in an effort to free himself as the swirling dust grew thicker in the turbulent air. Mr Corliss, gasping, strained to turn away, twisting against his entangled hands as he still fought to free them. A skein of fine red hair caught under his chin and tightened as he struggled against it, pulling him back against the jagged bricks, dragging his head painfully backwards into the void. From the distant cellars, over the sound of his own choking gasps, he perceived a most alarming sound. It was the sound of a woman coughing: the coughs growing worse and ever louder as the sound approached. His throat burned where the strands of hair were biting into it ever more tightly. As he thrashed and twisted his head from one side to the other he felt the hair somehow insinuating itself into his mouth and scratching at the back of his throat even as he coughed and choked against it. It was difficult to breath, or move his head forward at all. He could see only the darkness of the void as the coughing in the cellar grew louder and closer still.

Mr Corliss awoke in a panic: unable to stop coughing. There was another sound too that terrified him until he realised a moment later that it was the only the pounding of his own heart beating in his ears. At length, the coughing fit eased, only to begin again a few moments later.

CHAPTER THREE

Mr Corliss braced himself, cleared his throat and pulled himself up a little straighter as he entered the kitchen of Wakeley Hall: his head down. He had passed a dreadful night after waking from the nightmare, and the incessant coughing that had followed had allowed him little rest. All he wanted was to get down to the cellar and get on with his work. He did not wish to talk. Aside from anything else, he knew that talking would set him to coughing again, and coughing would only draw further unwanted attention his way.

"Morning, Mr Corliss," Mrs Gardiner began in a friendly tone.

He smiled and nodded, continuing on his way.

"Oh my word, Mr Corliss, you do look poorly. Are you feeling any better today?"

"Fine. Thank you," Mr Corliss whispered hoarsely, the back of his throat and his chest tensing as he felt the irritation building irresistibly in his airways. "It's nowt but a—" He turned away and covered his mouth with his hand as he was seized by deep prolonged coughing that he was helpless to stop. The blood rushed to his head and he squinted his eyes shut with the effort of trying to stop.

"Goodness me, you poor man," Mrs Gardiner tutted, motioning her young kitchen-maid Margaret to fetch a glass of water while Mr Corliss stifled the last cough into his palm. He was all too aware that it might begin again at any second.

"—Nowt but a cough," he croaked, forcing a smile as he accepted the glass of water and rapidly drank it down, blinking away the tears from his watering eyes.

Mrs Gardiner frowned. "I should watch that cough if I were you, Mr Corliss. It sounds right nasty. Perhaps you ought to see the doctor?"

Mr Corliss avoided meeting her eyes as he handed back the empty glass, merely nodding and smiling as he whispered, "Thank you."

The day's work proceeded to Mr Corliss' growing dissatisfaction, as his constantly having to stop to cough hampered his progress. He had no energy and wished only that he could lie down and go to sleep. He was beginning to feel troubled by just how unwell he felt. A dampness clung to his skin that the chill air of the cellar turned to an icy coldness that made him shiver. At other times he felt hot and light-headed and struggled to concentrate on his task.

More than once, as he stood, bent forward, his tools in his hands as another coughing fit came to its conclusion, something had compelled him to look over his shoulder in the direction of the broken wall behind him. His thoughts were not of the young woman in the wall, but of himself. *"Could I have caught something from that foul air when the bricks caved in? If she did have the consumption could I have caught it from breathing her air? Her last breath? I breathed in her last breath … The last scream from her lips is inside me … "*

As he stopped to rest again between tightening the screws in yet another of the endless shelves, it struck him that he could not remember the last time he had felt so ill. The feeling of painful irritation ran from the back of his mouth, down his airways and into his lungs. When he tried to take in a very deep breath his chest felt constricted and there was a dull pain right in the pit of his lungs. At least he didn't have to talk to anyone down here. But the sawdust also aggravated the feeling of irritation. Mr Corliss had grown so afraid of triggering another coughing fit that he had taken to tying his handkerchief over his mouth and nose whenever he had to use his saw or disturb the little piles of sawdust that had accumulated over the floor.

As he had no appetite, and less inclination for talk, he had not ventured upstairs for his lunch, and with the aid of his handkerchief serving to take the chill off the air as he breathed, he had managed at last to settle into some productive work, and to try to forget, for a few hours, the coughing and the worry that had plagued him all the morning. In his thoughts, he chided himself for fretting like an old woman over a little cough, and reminded himself of all the little colds and temporary ailments he had endured over his forty-eight years: all of which he had managed to survive.

"Aye, William," he rasped out loud to himself with a silent chuckle, "it will take more than a little cough to—"

An itching, burning spasm contracted the back of his throat and a seizure of deep coughing bent him forwards. Mr Corliss pulled the handkerchief from his face and turned away from the wall of shelves, worried that he might bump his head as the coughing contracted his long torso, neck and head forward with each rasping bark that wracked him. He tried to calm himself against the breathlessness he felt, and the alarming new sound his coughs now produced: an abrasively bass, animal-like braying at the bottom of each deep cough, as though the windpipe was beginning to collapse on itself each time, and the walls of the lungs and airways were grating against themselves with each unnaturally violent expulsion of air. His eyes streamed with tears as the fit continued, his brow contracted with discomfort and distress.

For a moment it seemed to be stopping and Mr Corliss struggled to swallow, to catch his breath without triggering another attack. But the painful spasm in his throat struck him again like a punch to the lungs that forced out all the air he had and pushed him forward again, his eyes involuntarily clenching shut.

It was then that he noticed it. Against the deep grey black of his closed eyelids there was an after-image in luminous blue-white that seemed burned into his inner sight. He strained to make sense of it as the coughing continued. If it had been the after-image of the bare electric light globe that hung from the vaulted ceiling, why did the shape look so ... curious? It had to be some kind of optical illusion. It had to be the after-image of the electric light-bulbs as it could be nothing else. He reasoned that was not accustomed to electric lighting, and down here in the gloomy cellar, it must have had some strange effect on his eyes.

Mr Corliss blinked open his eyes as the violent coughing went on, trying to clear the tears from his blurred vision. He was facing the hole in the wall and had been since the fit began. There was nothing there but a small moth circling in the dusty air. The horrible barking coughs went on, and Mr Corliss shook his head in exasperation, dropping his tools and rubbing his eyes with the palms of his hands. He shook his head again. When he closed his eyes, the after-image was there still, beside the negative image of the hole in the wall. But while the faint after-image of the hole in the wall disappeared almost at once, the other image remained undiminished. There was something about it that troubled him. The suggestion of its shape: somehow strangely like the figure of a person. But then, he reasoned, he did not know what shape the wire filaments in these electrical globes were. For all he knew, they might be that shape exactly.

He opened his eyes wide again, blinking the tears away furiously. There was nothing there. He focussed his efforts on stifling the spasm in the back of his throat and tried consciously to breathe only through his nose. At last the coughing subsided. He took a halting step towards the hole in the wall and closed his watery eyes once more. Nothing. Of course, there was nothing – no after-image except the jagged shape of the hole: faint and dissolving away to black in a second. Something touched his shoulder and he spun around with a shrill cry – finding only the alarmed face of Mr Parker behind him.

"Oh, my word, Mr Corliss! You look so unwell!"

Mr Corliss shook his head, stifling the irritation he felt in his throat. "Nowt but a cough," he rasped.

"I had meant to call in on you earlier, but we're still having trouble in the dairy you see, and we've all been rather busy … I don't like the sound of that cough, Mr Corliss. Have you been to see a doctor about it?"

"No, sir."

"Well, perhaps you ought to."

"Mr Parker … " Mr Corliss began than hesitated. Mr Parker nodded encouragingly, leaning in a little closer to hear the carpenter's rough whisper of a voice. "If that lass in the wall there did have TB like they were saying, it's not possible is it, that when the wall broke open and all that dust came out … ?"

Mr Parker straightened up, his eyes widening in distress at Mr Corliss' concerns. "Oh no! I shouldn't think so. No, I really don't think you need fear anything like that, Mr Corliss. Of course, I'm no doctor, but I would think it very unlikely that … No, I really don't think so. But why don't you go along to Mr Astley's doctor this afternoon and put your mind at rest. We shall pay for the consultation and any medicine you might need."

Mr Corliss dropped his chin and shook his head with an uneasy smile. "Nay, I couldn't, sir."

"No, I do insist, Mr Corliss, it's the least we can do for you after everything that's happened. I'm really dreadfully sorry for the worry this must have caused you. And if you need to take a day or two to recover –

whatever Dr Ronson recommends – I shall explain to Mr Astley. Will you do that for me, Mr Corliss?"

Mr Corliss nodded, a little relieved to be forced to do what he both wanted and feared to do. "Thank you, sir. Right good of you."

"Splendid." Mr Parker looked at his pocket watch. "Why don't you go along now, before Dr Ronson starts his afternoon surgery. If you tell him I sent you, I'm sure he will be able to see you at once." Mr Parker took a step back and surveyed the work that had been done so far. "All this is looking marvellous, Mr Corliss. It's coming along remarkably well. There's no urgency to any of this work, so please take whatever time you need to get better."

Mr Corliss nodded with embarrassment as he packed his tools back into their box, stifling a cough. His brow crinkled as a thought crossed his mind, and he stood up, his tool box clutched in his damp palm.

"Mr Parker?" he whispered. "Have you heard anything back, about the matter of … " Mr Corliss gestured gingerly in the direction of the jagged wall cavity.

"Ah," Mr Parker began, eyeing Mr Corliss cautiously, trying to gauge how much information to impart. "Yes." Mr Parker cleared is throat. "Yes, Mr Chandler from the Archaeological Society called in last night. It seems that the county coroner is in agreement with his initial assessment. The, ah, young lady, is indeed believed to have died in the time of the last Baronet, Sir Benjamin Stockard, just as Mr Chandler suggested."

"Oh aye," Mr Corliss frowned.

"Beyond that, I don't think it can be established exactly who she was or why … ah, how she ended up in such a dreadful predicament … but it was certainly, ah, foul play. She was alive when she was put into the wall, the poor creature." Mr Parker smiled sadly at Mr Corliss, then looked at the floor.

Mr Corliss nodded and turned to walk away, before halting. "And did they say," he croaked, clearing his throat. Mr Parker strained forward to hear as Mr Corliss strained to making himself audible. "Did they say if she had the consumption?"

"Ah," Mr Parker prevaricated, "well, in fact … the coroner did think it likely. It seems so, yes. But as I said, Mr Corliss, I really don't think you have anything to fear on that account. On a more uplifting note, ah, Mrs Astley has very kindly insisted that the young woman's remains be brought back to the undertakers here in the village once they are released by the coroner, so that they might receive a proper burial in the local churchyard, rather than in a pauper's grave in another town. Mr Chandler told us that that was the expected, ah, procedure, but Mrs Astley didn't think it fitting for a local, ah, resident to be buried that way and in another town. So, that's very kind of her … and Mr Astley, of course … once Mrs Astley had persuaded him of the idea." Mr Parker forced a smile.

Mr Corliss nodded, his eyes travelling from Mr Parker to the hole in the wall, as he turned to leave the cellar, the terrible deep coughing returning and echoing after him as he left.

CHAPTER FOUR

"You can put your shirt back on now, Mr Curtis." Dr Ronson took the stethoscope earpieces from his ears, and went to wash his hands in his basin.

Mr Corliss hurriedly pulled on his vest and shirt, fumbling to do up his buttons while tensing against the impulse to cough. There seemed little point in telling the doctor that he had been calling him by the wrong name throughout the consultation when even the thought of speaking made the back of his throat tense up. His felt his face colouring, tears coming to his eyes as the urge to cough overwhelmed him. The thought of making so much horrible noise before a man such as the doctor mortified him and made his throat tense tighter. He began to splutter then to cough in earnest, and the terrible barking braying noise persisted for some moments. Mr Corliss felt keen embarrassment at the horrible sound, and watched Dr Ronson's impassive back all the while as he struggled to regain his breath.

"Excuse me, Doctor," he whispered.

"Yes, it is a rather unpleasant cough," Dr Ronson observed coldly, peering at Mr Corliss over his gold-rimmed spectacles and resuming his seat behind the desk. "But as to the other question you mentioned: no, it is quite impossible for you to have contracted pulmonary tuberculosis in that

35

fashion. Quite impossible. Airborne droplets, Mr Curtis, spread the bacterium Mycobacterium tuberculosis. You wouldn't find any airborne droplets in a tomb, and even if you were to, the symptoms would not appear as quickly as this. No. We must not let our imaginations run away with us. What you have is a simple respiratory infection. Most often self-limiting in a healthy individual — that is to say, all being well it should go away by itself."

Mr Corliss nodded, his cheeks hot with a sense of his own foolishness. "I see."

"It is not unheard of for men in your trade to develop pulmonary problems later in life: constant exposure to saw-dust and other irritants, scarring of the lungs, higher susceptibility to pneumonia and so on … "

Mr Corliss' brow furrowed, suddenly recalling the wheezy old man who had worked in his master's workshop while he was a young apprentice. He had quite forgotten the old man's incessant coughing and his endless spitting into the sawdust on the floor until now. Dr Ronson began to write on his notepad, paying little heed to his patient.

"No evidence of anything like that here, of course, but one must expect to see a slightly higher incidence of respiratory problems in these occupations. No, Mr Curtis, you have what laymen call a 'bug,' and all you need is a day or two of rest, keep warm, plenty of fluids, and so on. Take this prescription to Mr Winfield in the high street and see that you take the cough medicine as directed. You'll be fine in a few days. And please try to refrain from diagnosing yourself with any other fatal illnesses in future. Best leave the diagnoses to me, hmm?"

Dr Ronson held out the narrow piece of paper to Mr Corliss, who was hastily tying his neck-cloth over his shirt collar. Dr Ronson noticed the missing tip of Mr Corliss' left hand ring finger and smiled smugly, his head tilted to one side.

"Another occupational hazard, I see – missing fingertips."

Mr Corliss stiffened and dropped his hands to his sides, curling his fingers into a ball to hide them. "Nay," he whispered. "That happened when I were a boy."

"Ah," Dr Ronson replied disinterestedly, searching for something in his desk drawer. "Well, good day to you, Mr Curtis. Please give my best regards to Mr Parker when next you see him."

Mr Corliss waited in a quiet corner of the chemist's shop, pretending to look at the various creams and bottles on the shelf nearby. He felt so foolish now that the doctor had dismissed his concerns, but he was greatly relieved, nonetheless, to know that his cough was perfectly ordinary. All he wanted now was to get his medicine and to go home without making a spectacle of himself with another loud coughing fit. He tried to ignore the pain in the back of his throat, to resist the itching irritation that tickled his airways with its scratchy fingers and to stay quiet and calm: but he had his handkerchief at the ready to muffle the coughing should it start.

"It's Mr Corliss, isn't it?" a woman's voice called out behind him.

He jumped and turned his head, triggering another fit of coughing that made him cover his mouth with the handkerchief at once. He felt his face colour and blinked away his tears as the concerned middle-aged woman stared at him, her fingers adjusting the scarf around her neck as she leaned back from the terrible noise Mr Corliss was making. He tried to place her as the coughing continued: her round face with its prominent nose and awkward smile looked familiar.

"It's Mrs Hargreaves," she explained. "You fixed some sticking doors for my husband last year."

Mr Corliss nodded and tried to smile, still keeping the handkerchief pressed to his mouth as the coughing subsided. His darting eyes swept the shop, registering the various looks of concern and distaste in the glances of the other customers as they stared at him.

"I heard you were the one that found that body up at the Hall," she ventured. "That must have been an awful thing?"

Mr Corliss stiffened at the probing of her morbid curiosity and the further attention that her voice was attracting from other quarters in the small chemist's shop. He gestured at his throat and tried to mime the words "Sorry. Lost my voice." He wiped the tears from his face as she took a step nearer. The corner he had been hiding in left him nowhere to retreat.

"They're saying that it was her who did for old Sir Benjamin and his family – is that true? That mad lass who deliberately gave them all the consumption?"

Mr Corliss felt sweaty and ill, and had to look away as he saw a couple of the other customers stepping closer, while others still craned their necks, pretending not to be interested. Mr Corliss could only shrug that he did not know. A plump young woman with an equally plump baby in her arms moved closer to Mrs Hargreaves.

"I heard she had red hair, just like in the story – she was supposed to be Scottish, wasn't she, Mrs Hargreaves?"

"Aye, that's what I was always told, Scottish … Eliza summat, wasn't it?"

"Eliza Burns," another customer answered.

"Aye, that's it!" Mrs Hargreaves exclaimed. "Eliza Burns. A wild, redheaded Scottish fury – and you actually saw her! How did she look, Mr Corliss? Was it frightening?"

"Our gran always called her a witch when she told the story," the second customer commented, jigging her baby gently up and down in her arms. "A spiteful witch with ideas above her station. If she couldn't steal Sir Benjamin away from his poor wife, no-one would have him – but to infect his wife and child and the household too … ooh, it fair makes my skin crawl."

"Well I can't think of much that's more evil than spreading diseases on purpose - and to a high-born family, a woman with child. Maybe your gran was right."

"Our gran usually was."

Mr Corliss wondered how the air in the shop had grown to hot and so thick: it was difficult to breath. Coughs seized him once more and the ugly bass braying that felt as though his lungs were collapsing and pressing flat immediately silenced the women's conversation that had sprung up around him. The woman with the baby rushed away, covering the baby's face. Mr Corliss blinked as tears filled his eyes and streamed down his hot cheeks. The coughing became an animalistic noise like a donkey at its ugliest pitch, and the increased force of the contractions in his chest made his eyes close tightly. There it was again, an after-image in glowing blue-white against the darkness of his closed lids. He tried to reason, as he continued coughing, that the light from the window had shone directly on Mrs Hargreaves as she spoke to him. That was why the luminous after-image looked so peculiarly like a woman – that was why it appeared larger and closer than it had before. Maybe all this coughing was hurting his eyes, straining them somehow and causing this strange effect.

"Mr Corliss!"

Mr Corliss blinked open his eyes and saw that Mr Winfield was calling him and holding out a bottle towards him, smiling gently from behind his counter. Mr Corliss strained to stop his lungs convulsing and winced at the burning sensation in the back of his throat.

"Ooh, you take care of that cough now, Mr Corliss," Mr Hargreaves encouraged from a distance of some yards. "It sounds right nasty."

Mr Corliss sat slumped in his chair before the fire, and turned the page of his book. His eyelids were red and heavy. What a pleasure it had been just to have some relief in the couple of hours since he had taken the cough syrup. His stomach muscles were sore from the day's coughing and his voice was almost gone. He put the book down for a moment and took up the bottle of cough syrup the chemist had given him, his eyes scanning the label for whatever ingredients it contained that had soothed his coughing so well. He nodded as he read the list: "Alcohol, Cannabis Indica, Chloroform, Heroin," and their respective amounts. Although his interests in books ranged widely, science had never been one of them, so he resigned himself to marveling at the effectiveness of the medicine without knowing precisely how it worked.

He picked up his book again, adjusting himself in the chair so that the glow of the fire was behind his left shoulder and perfectly illuminated the book as it rested on his knees. He had recognised a great deal of himself in Mr Wells' character of Kipps, the orphan taken in by elderly relations: although in his case it had been grandparents rather than an uncle and aunt. With a pang he thought of how he should have liked to open a bookshop too, just as Kipps planned to do. But it seemed to him that choices such as those came more freely to characters in stories than they did to real folk. Still, one could imagine what such a life might have been, had he been a more sociable man, with a loving wife by his side through all of life's travails.

Mr Corliss' head whipped forward as a cough burst from his lungs. His throat suddenly itched and ached again. He looked at the mantel clock. Mr Winfield had told him to take the medicine not more frequently than every four hours. It had only been three hours since he had first taken it. He weighed up the numbers in his mind and reasoned that it was probably better to wait another hour and take it just before bed. The better he slept, the better he would feel in the morning. His tea was still warm. Perhaps if he sat quietly and sipped at his tea as he tried to finish the book, he might not make himself cough too much before the hour came around.

He began to read from where he had left off, trying to distract himself from the rising scratching tickle he could feel in his airways. He put his finger under the sentence he was reading to try to focus his thoughts on it. His throat began to tense. He tried to make it relax. It was just a cough. In a day or two it would pass. *"Nowt to be worried about."* The sensation abated and he smiled, moving his finger under the next sentence. He heard a sound the seemed to come from outside, like a woman coughing, and his head spun towards the window behind him. The movement of his neck triggered a convulsion in his throat, forcefully punching the air from his lungs so that he lurched forwards: his book dropping to the floor. He coughed unceasingly: those same deep and bruising coughs with their ugly donkey bray. It seemed to be increasing in intensity and his eyes shut tight against the renewed force of the coughing.

There it was again. As he tried not to choke, tried to catch his breaths between the violent spasms of his lungs, the same luminous figure glowed spectrally behind his closed eyelids. He opened his streaming eyes, blinking furiously to try to clear his sight. The little room was empty and all the light was behind him. The fire's glow blended softly into the gloom of the darkened room – there was nothing here to create such a sharp after-image in his vision. The book he had been looking at was more or less square: its outline regular and even. Not like this … this spindly shape that appeared more defined now than it had been before. It had to be some trick of the light on his strained eyes.

The coughing struck him with renewed force and his eyes shut reflexively. Between gasps for air and sickening guttural bellows, he tried to make out the shape more clearly. It seemed perhaps a little larger than it had this afternoon, and the more he kept his eyes closed as he coughed, the clearer it became. Its shape was so like that of a woman, extremely frail and thin – indeed, he even fancied he could make out the outline of long trailing hair that curled from the bowed head down past the shoulders. Its head seemed tilted down, as though looking at the floor. He moved his head, shook it as he coughed, yet somehow the figure remained fixed in its place, as though he were looking at something that was actually standing there before him: as though it were standing some feet away on the worn old rug in the middle of the room.

He forced his eyes open again, rubbing at them with his hands, feeling the wetness of his tear-marked skin and wiping his wet palms on his shirt as he stared at the empty room before him with searching eyes. There was nothing there. How could there be? He was alone as he always was. The hacking cough went on and he could do little to make it stop. He closed his eyes deliberately. The iridescent shape remained standing before him. Now Mr Corliss stood up, raising his wearily convulsing frame: pushing himself up with his hands on the arms of his chair.

He kept his eyes closed and moved a step to the left. The figure remained as though fixed in its place on the floor and as he moved he could see it now almost from the side. There was no doubting now it had the shape of a small-framed woman, painfully emaciated, almost skeletal in a long trailing dress: a little over five feet tall. He could discern no detail in the luminous after-image other than the sharply defined outline. Yes, the chin appeared to be dropped onto the chest. The figure was as still as a statue, but as he moved it appeared to be somehow three-dimensional.

Mr Corliss stepped back to the right; the figure remained squarely facing him. Still coughing, he ventured a step forward. Another couple of steps forward and he would very close to the shape, almost looking down on it. He lifted his foot to move, his cough turning into a scream as the luminous figure appeared to move, to lift its face towards him.

Mr Corliss' eyes opened wide, wildly searching the space before him where the figure appeared to have been. Of course there was nothing there. How could there have been anything? He felt his brow, registering the cold sweat that clung to his hot skin. *"I have a fever. That's what it is."* Mr Corliss stifled the last gasps of his whimpering cough with his handkerchief and realised that he was trembling and felt like he was going to be sick. He shook his head, closed his eyes again. Nothing.

His throat burned terribly and his stomach muscles were very sore. *"Perhaps it's the cough medicine,"* he thought. *"That other cough medicine gave me nightmares last night. Likely this one is the same only stronger."* He had tried to forget his first glimpse of the glowing shape in the cellar of Wakeley Hall earlier in the day. It was easier to dismiss that time and the time in the chemist's shop as optical illusions of some kind. But this? Here in his own home, in the comfortable gloominess of his sitting room? "Perhaps *all the coughing really has done something to my eyes – and the cough mixture is making me imagine that it's ... a fever can make you hallucinate, like when you were little ... "*

He caught his breath and trudged into the kitchen, hesitating over the cupboard under the sink before opening it and pulling out a dusty bottle of sherry. He never touched drink in ordinary circumstances. The thought of his father had always been enough to erase any interest in it from his mind. He had only bought the bottle on the chance of anyone calling in unexpectedly. But of course no-one ever did. Only old Mr Watson from up the road sometimes, or one of the other tradesmen from the village when they wanted something: but they were usually happy with a cup of tea. *"Am I going mad? Am I seeing things? Nay, it's nowt but the fever and the medicine, that's all, and my eyes are sore and tired. My nerves are playing me up, that's all it is."*

He opened the bottle and poured a little into a cup. He could still feel his pulse pounding in his ears, but at least the coughing had subsided. He took a sip and closed his eyes again. Nothing – only blackness. He suppressed a wince at the unaccustomed taste of the drink, fearing that a sudden intake of the cold air in the kitchen might start the coughing again. He drained the cup and shuddered at the aftertaste and the smell of the alcohol that evoked some nebulous twinge in his heart. He quickly replaced the bottle in the cupboard and rinsed the cup in the sink. His skin was cold and clammy. He recalled having had a fever when he was young and some kind of delirium that held him caught between sleep and waking. It had seemed to go on forever before it had receded and things felt normal again. Perhaps this was something of that kind – a sort of waking dream caused by his fever?

He came back to the sitting room where the fire still burned reassuringly. Only his book lying on the floor was out of place. He closed his eyes again. The uninterrupted blackness reassured him somehow. He made ready for bed and brought the cough medicine into his room, setting it on his bedside table. He carried his candle over to the wash-stand in the corner and eyed himself in the mirror with alarm. He looked dreadfully ill. His eyes were red and swollen: his cheeks gaunt and ashen. "Oh, Willy-boy, you poor fellow," he croaked to his reflection quietly. "Never mind. Soon be better."

Another coughing fit seized him as he made his way to bed, careful to keep his eye on the shaking candle, lest he drop it or spill wax on the floor. An owl hooted hoarsely outside in the distance. He reasoned now how easily it might have been mistaken for a person coughing when he had heard it earlier.

Mr Corliss sat up in bed. He could not remember the last time he had felt so ill and so wretched ... so alone. He wondered what his life might have been like if he had married, if he had not run away from Miss Burrows with her claustrophobic interest in him and her awkward professions of love and all her plans for their life together. He coughed again for a minute or two and the effort of it exhausted him now beyond weariness. He poured out another measure of the cough medicine and eyed it warily, nervous now to take it down in case it was the cause of the thing he had imagined behind his eyes. He sighed and swallowed it, screwing up his face against the nasty taste. At least he would have a few hours relief, hopefully more. Some silly nightmares he could put up with, but he could not do without another night's sleep. And he had no cause to get up early in the morning so he could lie in and rest as long as he wished. He could finish *Kipps*, and maybe start on another book. He had a backlog enough of books he wished to read in the bookcase in the hallway.

He wrapped his woollen muffler around his neck and blew out his candle, staring into the low burning coals in the grate for a few moments before he eased himself down onto the pillows, relaxing as the medicine took hold and pulled him down into sleep.

Mr Corliss twisted and whimpered – sweating and wheezy – through uneasy hours of troubled sleep. Through endless unquiet dreams he was tormented by some vague task that he knew he must perform. Its exact nature was never clear to him, but the nebulous and dreadful consequences of his failing to do it hung always over his head like a great sword, ready to fall at any moment.

His pale lips moved, his upper lip drawing back in fear and repulsion. His croaking whisper broke the silence of the night as its troubled sounds at length formed audible words. "What do you want?" Mr Corliss coughed himself awake into the darkness, his eyes closed as he hacked and barked, sitting himself up to give full vent to the deep coughing. He started and cried out as the glowing white figure coalesced into shape once more behind his closed eyes: the fright of it making him choke and cough all the harder. Somehow it appeared a little closer than before.

He blinked open his swollen and sleepy eyes. The room was still dark save for the small glow of the burning coals low in the grate. He felt his alarm ease to see the room empty and calm, as it should be in the near dark of the early hours. *"It's only this fever,"* he thought as he rubbed at his damp face with his large and calloused hands. *"It's the fever and the cough medicine … and my eyes don't feel right … "*

As the coughing fit eased he leaned back wearily against the bed head. The muscles in his stomach ached from coughing, and his throat and airways burned. He frowned at the shapeless memory of his endless nightmare but could recall nothing of its substance save for some meaningless detail about carrying some large object and feeling terrified, not knowing where he could put it down. He peered at the little clock on the mantel, straining to make out the hour. It appeared to be about two a.m. *"So long until morning. So long until it's light."* Mr Corliss sighed, wincing as the scratching began to trigger his inflamed airways once more. He leaned forward, his elbows on his knees, as the coughing began again in earnest.

He noted with dismay that the coughing felt worse somehow, and was so alarmed by the nature of the wheezing breathless convulsion that seized him, he was unconscious of his eyes squeezing shut. He tried to pay no heed to the luminous spindly shape behind his eyelids as he struggled for breath against coughs so deep he thought he might vomit at the end of each terrible expulsion of air. Yet there it was still, unchanged, if perhaps a little clearer again in its outline: a few feet away from him, this ghastly and withered white female silhouette. Mr Corliss forced his eyelids open, blinking against the profusion of tears, and desiring only for the coughing to cease and to be reassured by the empty familiarity of his room. His head twitched at the suggestion of some movement in his peripheral vision that he at first took to be a stray cinder from the grate. The coughing persisted and the nauseating, burning retching of his lungs was beginning to make him feel weak and dizzy. He turned his head in the direction of the fireplace: his red eyes widening then blinking wildly. Something seemed to be further clouding his tear-filled vision – a subtle white blur as though something was in his eye – only it was in the very spot that the figure had seemed to occupy when his eyes had been closed. And now with his eyes wide open, it stayed in place even when he moved his head.

He rubbed at his eyes and blinked again. It was still there, like a breath of smoke in the air. Yes, it must be smoke, some stray wisp of smoke that had escaped that updraft of the chimney. Mr Corliss closed his eyes again as the coughing struggled on. He had not imagined it: the ghostly after-image behind his closed eyelids occupied the very same spot in the room as the cloudy grey patch in the air. He gave a little whimper of despair and turned to face the other wall as the coughing at last subsided. The bottle of Mr Winfield's cough medicine sat on the bedside table within easy reach. He stared at it a moment, weighing up which was worse: being awake or being asleep. He snatched up the bottle and took a swig from it without pausing to measure it into his spoon. He looked back nervously over his shoulder as he got his breath back. There was nothing there. All appeared as it should be. As he tried to calm himself and lowered his head back down onto the pillow, pulling the covers up over his head, he resolved not to turn back towards the fireplace again until the morning came.

Mr Corliss awoke a few hours later, wondering if he had not dreamt all the events of the night. His throat ached dreadfully and he felt terrible. Out of habit he rolled back towards the fireplace to check the mantle clock as it was still fairly dark outside. He stared at the space where he had thought or dreamed he had seen something that should not be there, hanging in the air, when he had awoken earlier. *"Must have been a dream."* He shook his head at the thought. It was just after five thirty. He rested his tired back against the headboard and glanced at the bedside table. The lid lay beside the bottle of cough medicine and a sticky black drop of the stuff had run down the side of the bottle and onto the table. The messiness of it disturbed him, but the implications of it disturbed him even more.

He furrowed his brow and put his hand to his throat, feeling the enlarged and tender glands under his jaw. Without a thought, he began to yawn and the shock of cold air hitting the back of his throat bent him double as his throat and lungs convulsed and all the air was squeezed out of him. Blood surged to his head as dizziness and nausea came in rising waves at the end of each deep, violent expulsion of air. Tears streamed from his eyes and he ducked instinctively as something appeared to loom beside him to the left of the bed. He reeled backwards, his lungs still convulsing, his body straining, sliding further back, his spine arched and his neck twisted: his eyes gaping in horrified disbelief to see a smoky figure coalescing into the half-light before the fire as his coughing raged on.

The outline that had burned itself into his memory now filled out before his blazing eyes, and all at once, through his tears, he saw clearly the spindly form of a woman, glowing a spectral translucent blue-white in the gloom. Her limbs were skeletal. Her curling hair was sparse. She wore the remnants of a tattered gown of an antique design. Mr Corliss was bent back over the side of the bed, the side of his face hitting the front of the bedside table as the coughs continued to seize him helplessly. He could now see the downcast face clearly as the figure stood very close to the other side of the bed. He could only cough out the cry that the sight of her rent from his heart. Huge empty eye-sockets gaped blackly down from a bony face with skin like old parchment. He could see the bones of the chest partly exposed. The nose looked sharp, the mouth, at first closed, now fell open. A terrible hollow windy whistling cough came from the mouth, in time with his own coughing.

Mr Corliss slid backwards from the bed, scrambling to his feet on the floor as he fled the room, slamming the door behind him. He could barely breathe for coughing; could barely stand for the dizziness that seemed to squeeze at his consciousness. He ran to the parlour, to the kitchen, not knowing what to do. He threw open the kitchen door and ran outside into the freezing and dark morning. The convulsive coughing came on again and his body bent forward, his hands squeezing his knees with painful pressure as he tried to stay conscious for lack of air; tried not to vomit with the deep retching in his lungs that punctuated every braying cough. His eyes looked at the ground, burning, weeping, as a pair of small bare feet, white and bony beneath the shreds of a long gown, coalesced on the dark earth in the morning gloom. There it stood in the same position as he had seen it in the bedroom – in the corner of his left eye. He heard a second echoey cough wheezing in time with his own.

His heart hammered in his chest. He did not dare to raise his eyes at the terrible thing before him. Mr Corliss span around and raced back inside, bolting the door behind him. He peered through the kitchen window into the yard. Outside, all was silent and still. Not even a bird moved. His feet on the wooden kitchen floor felt like ice. His sweat felt frozen to his goosebumped flesh. In between coughs he shivered ferociously in his sweat-dampened pyjamas.

His eyes darted around the room. He was quite alone: alone in a way he had not felt since he was a boy. No-one could help him then. No-one was here with him now. He took up a tea-towel from its holder on the edge of the sink and held it over his mouth, desperate to stop the coughing if he could find any way. It did seem to help. With the painful chill taken off the air by the cloth, he managed at last to subdue the coughing fit. He paced around the small kitchen, unable to stand still and trying to get his jangling nerves in hand. His heart was still beating so fast he worried for a moment that might have a heart attack. It was hard to breathe normally. For a second he thought of running to old Mr Wilson's house up the road – but what would he say to Mr Wilson? How could he tell of the things that were happening without sounding mad? It *was* mad. What else could it be but madness to see such things – to imagine such horrors as these? What would the old man do anyway but talk endlessly of the old days as he loved to do. How could old Mr Wilson help? How cold anyone help if the problem was inside his own mind?

"*Get warm,*" an inner voice instructed him with calming certainty. Mr Corliss nodded to himself, still holding the cloth over his mouth. Nervously he went to the parlour, hesitating in the doorway and checking that the room was empty before going in and restarting the fire. He crouched before the fire, wrapping the knee rug from his armchair around his hunched shoulders. Mr Corliss continued to shiver as he stared into the burning coals of the fire. A thought occurred to him that gave him some tiny sliver of consolation. "*It can't get into the fire … as long as I look into the fire, I won't see it,*" he thought, as he felt the spasm in his airways itching again.

On his knees, with his arms crossed over his chest, clutching the blanket around his heaving chest, he began to cough again and to cry. Keeping his eyes fixed on the fire he tried to tell himself that he must still be caught in his fevered dreams. If only he could wake up, if the fever broke, he might be all right again. From a few steps behind he heard a sound: a second cough, whistling and echoey, braying and wheezing in time with his own.

"What do you want?" he cried in a breaking and breathless rasp in between the wrenching spasms of his lungs: his eyes sore and his face hot as he stared unblinkingly into the fire.

The second cough echoed behind him once more, but now falling out of time with his own. He marshalled all his scant strength to hold his breath, to be silent for a moment if only he could, feeling his face grow red from the breathless strain. The second voice formed a whisper like a low whistling wind and the terrible moaning whisper formed a word:

" ... *Him* ... "

CHAPTER FIVE

Mr Corliss shivered. It was barely seven a.m. and he had pulled up his cart under the tall hornbeam tree whose partly denuded branches provided less shelter to his old mare, Peggy, than he might have wished. The overcast sky seemed intent on rain. He had dressed himself as warmly as he could and had wound his woollen scarf around his neck and face to try to stave off the irritating effects of the cold autumn air.

His brown plaintive eyes stared out from under his flat cap at the dark green painted door of Dr Ronson's cottage, which also housed his surgery.

"What can I tell him? What can I say that will not make me sound mad? But what if I am going mad? Oh Willie-boy, what are we to do? What are we to do?"

Mr Corliss put his head in his hands. Fear had forced him from his house after the terrors of the early morning. He had hoped that out in the open everything would be back to normal. He had hoped that the shock of the cold air might break his fevered delirium. He had hoped that doing something as ordinary as driving his docile old horse Peggy along familiar roads would prove to him that the events of the night had been nothing but a strangely vivid nightmare. But even Peggy seemed jumpy and nervous, throwing back her head and shying off suddenly to the side in her traces as she had never done before. It was always to the right, Mr Corliss had noted with a sinking feeling in the pit of his stomach, as if something on her left side were spooking her.

He had taken another dose of the cough medicine before he had left the house – feeling that he had to try something and not knowing what else to do – but still the cold air had caught in the back of his throat as he urged Peggy down the road away from his house. It was after about five minutes on the road that the first serious coughing attack had seized him. Mr Corliss tried to keep his gaze fixed on the road ahead in the low early morning light. As the worst of the coughing began he felt his eyes close reflexively and was relieved that the place in his field of vision that the ghostly figure had last occupied now seemed clear. Perhaps the nightmare had ended.

With his eyes still closed as the terrible coughs went on, he felt an impulse to turn his head – an impulse which some other part of his mind warned him he must not do. Yet something compelled him, as he sat, hunched forward on the well worn seat of his cart, to turn his head, ever so slightly, to the left. Against the soft blackness of his closed eyelids a luminous white shape intruded its spindly form. On the floor of the cart, where his closed eyes were directed, rested the glowing scrawny shapes of two bony bare feet, next to where his own feet rested.

Choking on his coughs, sick and dizzy for want of air, he allowed his closed eyes to move up only a fraction. The tatters of a long antique dress covered bent skeletal knees, the lower part of a withered form sitting motionless on the seat right beside him. He dared not open his eyes. He dared not look upon it again. All Mr Corliss could do was to turn his head away, coughing, and shaking the reins to spur Peggy on to the doctor's house, as a second voice echoed in its own coughs into his left ear.

"Are you prone to weakness of the nerves, Mr Curtis?"

Mr Corliss shook his head, his eyes downcast, as he pulled his jacket back on.

"Well," Dr Ronson sighed wearily, smoothing back his thinning hair, that was still uncombed after Mr Corliss had disturbed his morning's sleep. "It is conceivable, although not common for some men to have a bad reaction to certain medicines. Would this explain your hallucinations? I am not entirely sure that it would."

Mr Corliss frowned. He was relieved at least that the swig of cough mixture he had taken on the road had halted the coughing, but he could still not bring himself to look to his left side, even while he was able to breathe normally. He kept his eyes down and to his right side, a hot feeling of shame rising up inside him as he anticipated the direction the doctor's comments were about to take.

"Now as I understand it, you suffered a severe shock the other day. Very well. The sight of a dead body is often very distressing to a layperson who has not seen a deceased person before."

"Oh, but I h—" Mr Corliss began to say, but his whisper of a voice went unheard as Dr Ronson went on.

"—Certainly, from what I understand, the circumstances were not pleasant. One can understand how distressing such a discovery might be. But to give way to one's nerves, Mr Curtis, is to risk a descent into incipient decay of the brain and possibly even insanity. I wonder if you are something of an imaginative man, Mr Curtis. Am I right? Do you enjoy ghost stories, fanciful novels, romantic ballads, things of that nature?"

Mr Corliss could only shrug, unsure of what answer to give, or what answer might condemn him.

"For a strong-minded man, these interests do little harm, and certainly the right kind of literature is known to be very improving to a sound mind. But for those whose nerves are weak, I fear it can be quite unhealthy to give too much sway to the imagination and to fanciful ideas. I will prescribe you a tonic for your nerves, Mr Curtis, but fundamentally, it remains up to you not to give in to these flights of fancy and descents into nervous hysteria. You must cleanse your mind of these morbid fancies before they take hold and overmaster your reason. You did well to come to me now at the first signs and I think that shows that you do wish to overcome this mental weakness. I would advise you – when this little cough has cleared up of course – to try to take up some healthier pastimes: fishing, the village cricket club, bell ringing, things of that sort to get you out of the house and mixing with normal people. Will you try to do that?"

Mr Corliss nodded. "Thank you, Doctor."

Dr Ronson scribbled something down on his prescription pad and rose from his chair, extending his arm towards the door. Mr Corliss hastened to his feet and moved past the doctor towards the threshold.

"Of course, if matters progress, there are specialist doctors, and even hospitals for extreme nervous cases, but I am confident that with the right attitude, we can avoid all of that."

Mr Corliss nodded, clutching his cap in his hands, his back to the closed front door, as Dr Ronson handed him the folded prescription. Something caught Dr Ronson's eye, and he squinted towards the fine net curtains that covered the narrow glass panels on either side of the door.

"For heaven's sake, Mr Curtis," he chided, "I shouldn't let your wife sit out there in an uncovered cart in this rain – not unless you want her to catch her death."

Mr Corliss' head tilted back as the blood drained from it and sank with a hot surge to his heart. "My ... wife ... ?" he whispered breathlessly.

"Yes," Dr Ronson scowled at him, pointing towards the carriage under the hornbeam tree across the road. "Dressed like that, in this weather? Did you drag her out of the house in only her nightgown?" Dr Ronson tutted and shook his head in consternation and opened the door, looking at his watch. "Have her wait inside next time."

"I am not mad. Not mad!" Mr Corliss climbed up into the seat of the cart, careful not to touch the seat to his left. *"He saw her. She is real. He saw her!"*

He pulled his scarf up again over his mouth and nose, restlessly fidgeting and shifting in his seat as he tried to think. Tears sprang to his eyes with the relief that coursed through his heart. *"He saw her."* A thought froze him in place and his face suddenly fell. *"He saw her … She is real … she is real … she is real and she has attached herself to me … "*

Huddled against the drizzling rain, Mr Corliss drove Peggy on over long and empty country back roads. As the hours passed, the heavy grey clouds overhead did little to dispel the gloom of the morning. He could still not look directly at the seat beside him, but he had glimpsed enough in the periphery of his sight, when the coughing fits came on him, to feel increasingly oppressed and terrified by the constant presence of this phantom other.

At last he drew Peggy to a halt, taking another swig of the cough medicine before steeling himself to alight. He was a frequent enough visitor to the Thornedale public library to be on friendly terms with the librarian, Mr Crossley, but he scarcely knew what he should say to the kindly old gentleman today.

Mr Corliss entered the quiet building gingerly, pulling his muffler down to his chin, not sure where to look.

"How do, Mr Corliss?" a familiar voice called out from behind a desk.

Mr Corliss gave a thin smile and nodded at the pink-faced bald man in spectacles.

"Oh my word! You look right poorly! Whatever is the matter?"

Mr Corliss could only gesture to his throat and try not to cough as his concerned acquaintance looked him over and shook his head.

"Nowt but a cough," Mr Corliss was able to whisper.

"Oh deary me. And you've come all this way in the rain? You know I wouldn't begrudge you an overdue book in these circumstances, Mr Corliss!" Mr Crossley smiled warmly, his twinkling eyes still narrowed with concern. "I'd never give you a fine for that!"

Mr Corliss did his best to smile. He swallowed hard to try to clear his throat.

"Would you have," he strained to make his ragged voice audible, "any books on the history of Wakeley Hall? Or any books about … ghosts, Mr Crossley?"

"Wakeley Hall?" Mr Crossley pretended indignation. "There's not much call for books about Wakeley here in Thornedale, no indeed. We can't be doing with Wakeley books around here." The old gentleman winked good-humouredly. "But I'm sure I can find something for you, if you really must read about such an inferior place … aye, and ghosts too, if you've a mind for such things. Let me check my cards … "

Mr Corliss did his utmost not to cough, or not to cough too violently, as he sat in the silent library, searching indexes and scanning pages for the information he sought. At the sight of a movement in his periphery on the left side, Mr Corliss jumped and set himself coughing again.

"Ooh, forgive me, Mr Corliss," Mr Crossley soothed in a quiet tone as he touched Mr Corliss on the left shoulder. "Are you finding what you're after there?"

Mr Corliss screwed up his face, reluctant to speak, lest the coughing return and with it, an unwelcome occupant for the empty seat beside him at the table.

"Only it occurred to me that your particular interest today could have summat to do with a story I heard this morning about summat that happened at Wakeley Hall the other day."

Mr Corliss braced himself for the onslaught of morbid questions he dreaded.

"They found an old skeleton bricked up in the Hall from way back, I heard. Is that true?"

Mr Corliss could only nod, fearful of revealing his connection to the incident.

"Aha! Well now I understand your curiosity. Do they know who it's supposed to be?"

Mr Corliss strained to suppress the itching in his throat, contriving not to appear too interested in the story. "Someone connected to Sir Benjamin Stockard," he croaked. "The last Baronet, I heard … "

"Hmm," Mr Crossley mused, pursing his lips. "Well, this shall be very interesting, won't it? Yes, indeed." Mr Crossley raised his unkempt eyebrows.

Mr Corliss stared at him questioningly, not grasping the loaded tone of Mr Crossley's remark.

"Ah, well, you haven't been in the area all that long, Mr Corliss, so perhaps you don't realise: Wakeley and Thornedale don't see eye to eye over a good many things, and the reputation of good old Sir Benjamin is one of them. I know folk see him as some kind of martyred saint over your way, but it's not so here. Don't believe all the stories told of the Stockards in Wakeley."

Mr Corliss held his breath and urged Mr Crossley with his eyes to continue.

"Well the man you really ought to talk to is Reverend Booth up at the vicarage by the old church: he's quite the local historian in his way. It were he who mentioned the body to me when I bumped into him at the post office this morning. He collects all this local folk-lore you see, when he's not in here disagreeing with over his Greek philosophers and whatnot."

Mr Corliss stiffened at the thought of going to talk to a reverend, let alone one he had never even met. "Oh, I'm sure these books will be fine," he whispered.

"History is written by the rich and powerful," Mr Crossley mused, looking around the shelves of the library. "It's their side of things you'll find in all these books, like as not. Just like in Wakeley, you'll hear the toffs' version of things, because it were their village and everyone looked up to them. No, Mr Booth's your man if you want to hear another side to a story. And don't be shy of him, Mr Corliss. I know he comes over a bit grand and he's a man of the cloth and all, but he puts his strides on one leg at a time, just like the rest of us."

"Nay, nay, I wouldn't like to bother him with my idle curiosity," Mr Corliss demurred.

"Bother?" Mr Crossley laughed. "Nay, any excuse to get talking about local stories and he's off, is our Reverend Booth. You just try stopping him – he'll have you there all afternoon, Mr Corliss, so he will."

In his mind, Mr Corliss had immediately decided that he would not, could not, seek out Reverend Booth. It was simply impossible. But as he searched again through endless pages in the library books that Mr Crossley had found for him, it became clear that the story told in the books was the same as the story he had heard at Wakeley Hall with very little embellishment, save for dates, and the additional information of the names of Sir Benjamin Stockard's wife and other members of the family and household.

Of the woman who had brought them to their horrible demise little was said, save for her name: Eliza Burns. Nor could the books agree on her fate, with one saying that she had been imprisoned and died in a jail far distant from Wakeley, while another stated that she had been tried and hanged but did not say when or where. It was a wild and unrequited passion for a man high above her station that had driven the consumptive young woman mad, the books agreed, and having no hope of winning what she desired, she chose instead, in her madness, to destroy him and all that he loved.

Mr Corliss grew increasingly restless, both at the uselessness of what little information he had found, and at the thought of the nature of this thing that had seemed to attach itself to him. To what end? And why him? What more vengeance could she seek than the destruction she had already wrought on the Baronet? How could he free himself from something he could not touch: something that should not be – that could not, by any reasonable explanation, even exist? He thought again of Miss Burrows and how he had run away from her, moved to Wakeley just to escape from her cloying affection and all that she wanted from him. *"Am I being punished? Does Eliza Burns want to destroy me, like she destroyed him?"* He clutched at his throat and shook his head.

The perturbation in Mr Corliss' mind grew and with it the increasing irritation and itching in the back of his throat. The cough medicine was beginning to wear off, and other patrons had come into the library while his head had been buried in his books. It was growing ever harder to keep his coughing to the subdued, mouth-closed, occasional coughs he was trying so hard to muffle. More than once, the sharp-looking younger man with spectacles at the next table had stared at him pointedly for the noises he was making. Now the two older ladies at the end of his table began to stare as well. Mr Corliss gathered up a couple of the library books to take with him and rose from his chair as the coughing struck him again with full force. The older ladies whispered to each other, and he made the mistake of looking towards them, at the left hand end of the table, as they eyed him with distaste and one covered her mouth with a handkerchief. It was there again, the briefly glimpsed white form by his side that made him twist his head away and almost run towards Mr Crossley's counter.

Choking and scarcely able to breath as the coughing wracked him, he dropped the books in front of the startled librarian, who hastened to use his stamp and file his tickets, while Mr Corliss hacked and barked, bent double and eyes weeping, before him.

Mr Corliss' face reddened from want of air and the heat of disapproving eyes boring into him. Behind his coughs he could hear the second voice coughing again, quietly at first, but growing ever louder, as if it were moving closer behind him. He whimpered aloud at the faint suggestion of something brushing his left arm as it hung at his side: something feathery that might only have been a breath of wind from the open window. But he could not look, he dare not, any more than he could raise his eyes to the other patrons' disapproving stares. He clenched his fists and shuffled his feet, wanting only to run but unable to move while he struggled so hard for air. Mr Crossley pushed the hurriedly stacked books towards him and leaned back in his seat with evident aversion, his eyes darting apologetically towards his other patrons and back to Mr Corliss.

Mr Corliss could only nod, his cheeks burning as much as his throat did.

"You take care of that cough now, Mr Corliss," Mr Crossley whispered as his head gestured Mr Corliss towards the door.

Out in the light rain of the overcast day, Mr Corliss walked around his cart in an agitated circle, shoving the library books under a covering in the back of the cart. What was he to do? At his approach, Peggy began to shake her head and puff nervously, jangling her harness as he untied her bridle from the post to which he had tethered her. Still coughing, he climbed into the driver's seat and took another mouthful of the cough syrup: trembling with cold and the suggestion that the thing might have touched him – that it might be able to touch him again. He shook his head more violently, trying to shake the thought away. He could not stand to be touched, least of all by something such as she: something he could not escape, nor fight off. He put his head in his hands, covering the side of his left eye with his palm, as the coughing began to subside.

How could he possibly talk to this reverend? Even if it was the only hope he had of finding some answers, Mr Corliss simply did not know how he could go through with such a thing. He had always been paralysed around people in authority, ever since he was a boy. He thought as he grew older it would become easier, but nothing had changed: the fear of judgement, punishment, disapproval still rendered him as helpless as a child. To go to this man's house – a vicarage no less – and try to introduce himself, without coughing, without blushing, and to ask for an audience with him … *"Why are you so weak?"* Mr Corliss castigated himself. *"Why are you so afraid of everybody? Can't you just this once pretend to be like everybody else and just have a normal conversation with someone?"* He punched himself in the leg with his balled up fist, his teeth clenched hard. *"What is wrong with you? What has always been wrong with you? He will think you a fool. He will think you have lost your mind."*

Mr Corliss had stopped his cart under a sheltering tree across the road from the vicarage. He had gone as far as stepping down from the seat to stand on the ground beside the cart, but could not force himself to go any further. He could see a light in the window of one of the rooms of the vicarage. Someone was in. *"But it's not necessarily himself. He might be out. He is probably a very busy man."*

At least here in the shade of the tree he was not too visible, and there were no other houses, nor people, close by to see him loitering there, afraid to go further. He had never been a religious man. But now, as he stared at the towering church steeple beyond the vicarage, he wondered. Would a priest know how to free a man from the entangling arms of a phantom? Or would such a man merely think him insane? He knew he could not ask – could not tell the reverend about the spectre – but what if the reverend could see it, as the doctor had? *"And what if he thinks I am evil? Unclean?"*

Mr Corliss turned to face the other direction, his right hand gripping the side of the cart as he stared back up the road he had come from. *"I can't do it. I simply can't go in."* He began to cough again. He knew he should be in bed – he felt so desperately ill and tired, so weak. The strain was too much. He stooped, his head bent forward as the horrible coughing ground away at his lungs and airways. He fished out his handkerchief from his left hand pocket and covered his mouth with it to try to mute the grating sound: his head turned to the right, trying desperately not to look to his left, not wanting to see the thing that he could hear once more, coughing in time with him. *"How will it end? How can it end?"*

He leant his head into the crook of his right arm and wondered if he should pray to God for help. The second cough behind his own growing louder, nearer, as if drawing closer to his left ear. His skin turned to gooseflesh as he felt something nearing.

"Oh leave me alone!" he cried aloud as he coughed, half-choking on his words and beginning to cry.

Something touched his arm, lightly, like the touch of small and gentle fingers resting on his sleeve. Mr Corliss' head spun, his eyes widening to see two women standing beside him: one nebulously white and hollow-eyed; the other pink-cheeked, her hand warm and real upon his arm, her concerned eyes gazing into his own. His pained and blood-shot eyes rolled back behind fluttering swollen lids and with a rasping sigh, he collapsed to the ground.

CHAPTER SIX

Mr Corliss screwed up his face and shook his head at the taste of alcohol in his mouth.

"There, he's coming round," a deep male voice said softly.

A cool hand touched his brow. "Hmm, he has a bit of a fever, I think," a woman's voice answered.

Mr Corliss twitched and blinked open his eyes, his gaze darting sheepishly from the kindly face of the pink-cheeked woman leaning over him, to an older bespectacled man with curling black-grey hair like steel wool.

"There ... feeling better?" the woman asked, holding out a glass of brandy to him in her delicate white hands.

Mr Corliss nodded, unsure of what to say or where to look. He noted that he was lying on a fine sofa in a cosy parlour before a warming fire. The man with steel wool hair wore a clerical collar and was perched forward in his armchair: his expression caught somewhere between friendliness and worry.

"Have you been unwell?" the reverend enquired, peering at Mr Corliss over the top of his spectacles.

Mr Corliss took another sip of the brandy and coughed a little at the fumy taste. "Bit of a cough, that's all, Reverend," he whispered hoarsely, feeling frightened and embarrassed. "I've seen the doctor, it's nowt serious."

"You seemed very distressed when I came upon you outside," the lady observed gently, taking a seat on a chair close by the sofa. There was something in the kindness of her smile that made Mr Corliss fear he was about to weep, to tell all that he was suffering, and all that he had seen. He swallowed and looked away.

"I ain't been sleeping well, ma'am, what with the coughing," Mr Corliss tried to explain as his hosts leaned in to hear his ghostly voice. "I shouldn't have come out today I know, in this weather, only ... "

The reverend raised his eyebrows in some intrigue, straightening in his armchair. He was very tall and broad-chested. His face was broad and his skin swarthy. Pale blue eyes peered searchingly, keenly, from behind round gold-rimmed spectacles. A small gold cross hung from a chain around his neck. Mr Corliss blinked and looked at the floor, trying not to lose what nerve he could muster.

"Only, it were you I had hoped to see, Reverend. Ah, Mr Crossley suggested I should see you."

Reverend Booth looked at his wife and gave an almost imperceptible nod of his head. Mrs Booth, accustomed to her husband having visitors with private matters of the heart and soul to discuss, understood the signal at once and rose to excuse herself.

The reverend sat back in his chair, his large palms open and extending out to the sides. "How may I help you, Mr ... ?"

"Corliss, sir. William Corliss." Mr Corliss attempted to smile, but could barely look the imposing gentleman in the eye.

"Well, Mr Corliss, what may I do for you? I perceive that you have come some distance today."

"Aye, sir, it's from Wakeley that I've come, and it's Wakeley business that I wanted to ask you about."

Something glinted in the eagle-like eyes of the reverend, his finger resting upon his lips.

"Well, sir, I wanted to ask you ... that is, I was curious to know ... " Mr Corliss moistened his parched lips, wary of showing too much interest in the matter. "Mr Crossley said you know about local history – things that aren't written down in books ... only I was curious about the Baronets of Wakeley Hall ... ah, Sir Benjamin in particular ... and what happened to him."

Reverend Booth's expansive hand stroked his prominent and angular jaw, some thought formulating in his mind.

"Are you by any chance a carpenter, Mr Corliss?"

Mr Corliss' eyes widened in alarm and he struggled to suppress a cough, terrified that it would begin again. He screwed his eyes shut with the effort and nodded. Suddenly he felt ashamed of his workman's clothes and his worn shoes as they rested on the reverend's fine sofa with its dark cerise velvet upholstery.

"Was it you, Mr Corliss, who made that terrible discovery at Wakeley Hall the other day?" Reverend Booth leaned forward, his palms pressed together and his index fingers touching his lips in suppressed excitement.

Mr Corliss' mouth opened, but no sound came out as he struggled to think what to say. He nodded, staring at the reverend with suspicion in his swollen eyes. "How did you know?"

Reverend Booth dropped his gaze to the floor and smiled gently. "Well, Mr Corliss, it isn't every day that I get a visitor coming to my door to ask about Wakeley Hall, least of all one who has come so far under clearly trying circumstances and in such inclement weather. I can only deduce that your interest in the matter must be ... of a personal and pressing nature?"

"Aye ... it is at that."

"And they think that the poor young woman you found was Eliza Burns, from the old story, is that correct?"

"Aye, so they reckon." Mr Corliss blinked and stared into the flames of the fire. "I just want to know, what really happened ... to think of someone being bricked up like that ... I just want to know why, Reverend, if you can tell me owt about it."

"I understand, Mr Corliss. It must have been a dreadful thing for you to find – a frightful shock for you. From what I heard, the young woman was bound, tied up and bricked into the wall alive. Is that how it was?"

Mr Corliss gave a nodding blink that was almost a twitch.

"And she had red hair? There were still traces of hair, were there not? Red and curling?"

Mr Corliss swallowed and nodded again, feeling some little ease in his breast as the brandy soothed his nerves a little. "Aye," he answered quietly. "Red hair with a silver hairpin with a sort of bee on it."

Reverend Booth's upper body jolted forward, his hand reaching out searchingly towards Mr Corliss. "A bee? Did you say a bee?"

Mr Corliss stopped himself, aware that he had revealed too much: told something he ought not to know.

"Now that is most interesting." Reverend Booth's eyebrows raised and a sly smile played over his features before he composed them again. "Yes, a most telling detail. Anything else? Were there any other features you noted, Mr Corliss?"

Mr Corliss shook his head, aware that he had so far unwittingly answered more questions than he himself had asked. He felt uncomfortable and wondered if he should not leave before Reverend Booth extracted more information from him that he did not wish to impart.

"Well now, Mr Booth. With that one detail, I fancy you have settled a question that has hung in the air over Wakeley and Thornedale these past two centuries … I take it you are familiar with the story told in Wakeley of the good Sir Benjamin and the unbalanced young maid who was possessed by a singular and destructive obsession for him – is that what you have heard?"

"Aye, sir." Mr Corliss felt his heart beating faster. He tried not to permit himself to tremble.

"He was unwittingly victimised by this deranged Eliza Burns, he and his unfortunate family, until her mad scheme to infect them all was discovered, and Sir Benjamin had her sent away to prison, before he too followed his wife and child into the grave – is that not so?"

Mr Corliss nodded and swallowed, a pulse in his head pounding through his temples as he leaned towards Reverend Booth.

"Yes, that is the story told in Wakeley: the story that was told by Sir Benjamin, and then retold by his friends and the good people of Wakeley after his death. But there is another story … the story told by a terrified young woman who fled here to Thornedale in 1743. Eliza Burns had a sister, you see: a younger sister who also worked at Wakeley Hall farm. They had come down from Scotland together seeking employment, two years before the tragedy unfolded: Eliza and Bonnie Burns."

Mr Corliss furrowed his brow, his head shaking in incomprehension. "A sister?"

"Yes. Eliza was fifteen, and Bonnie two years her junior. They were orphans: their parents had been killed in an accident on the farm where they worked when a wagon had overturned, and their laird had thrown the girls out of the cottage the family had occupied on the estate. Seeking a better life they followed the mop fairs down to this part of the world and were pleased to find positions in such a picturesque and noble seat as Wakeley Hall."

Mr Corliss realised that he was holding his breath.

"With her bright red hair and her pale skin, Eliza stood out from the other girls, and it was not long before she came to the attention of Sir Benjamin. Eliza, being young and unworldly and tender-hearted did not see Sir Benjamin's well-practiced flatteries and attentions for the callous game that they were."

Mr Corliss stared into the dancing flames of the fire, his hand covering his mouth; pain in his eyes.

"Sir Benjamin gradually gained her trust, and by his flattering attentions, he began to kindle some spark in her young heart. When he saw that he was winning her over, he persuaded her to wait for him each night up by the ruins of Toubroneaux Priory on the windy hilltop at the edge of the moors. It is a picturesque enough spot in spring and in summer when the heather blooms as pink as a blush over the hills. But in winter it is a lonely and blighted place, and the roofless ruins of the priory afford little shelter from the wind that blasts up from the moors. And it was there when the heather was in full bloom that she waited every night for him – for he told her that he could never be sure when he could get away, unnoticed by his wife, to meet her. It was there that he seduced her and took her innocence. It was there that he professed to love her and promised to run away with her and marry her, giving her some trinket or other as 'proof' of his intentions. And she believed him.

"She loved him with all the fierce and passionate devotion of first love, and she believed that he loved her with the same devotion. And it was there, as spring chilled into winter, that he grew bored of her loving looks and her questions of how soon they might run away together. He had won her heart too well. The love she bore for him was more than he wanted. She wanted to possess him completely – not to share him with his wife. He told her it was getting harder for him to get away unnoticed in the evenings but that she should still wait for him. It was there that she continued to wait in the bitter winter cold as he forgot her. The more he pulled away from her the stronger her desire grew to possess him, to win him back. She had nothing else in this world of her own. All that she had, all that she dreamed life could give her, was tied up in her increasingly desperate quest to possess the great love that had been promised to her and taken away."

Mr Corliss blinked away the hot tears he felt coming to his eyes.

"She had by then discovered that she was with child. She thought he would be glad, she thought he would at last run away with her, if only he knew about the baby, but he never came to the priory anymore, where she still waited for him every night, yearning for him with all desperate and undying passion in her young heart. And when she saw him riding by the dairy and tried to approach him, to tell him that she loved him still with all her heart and begged to know what she had done to so displease him, and how she could win back his favour, he pushed her away with his boot. She fell, and the baby was lost … "

"Nay," Mr Corliss whispered sadly, shaking his head.

"It was as she recovered from the loss that the fever seized her and she began to take ill with consumption. It was the cold you see – all those long nights she waited alone at the priory as winter closed in with little but a thin shawl to protect her. Bonnie said that some part of her sister died with the baby – as if all the sweet innocence in her nature had simply been extinguished. But despite everything her love for Sir Benjamin would not die. All that remained for her was the fierce passion that still burned in her breast to possess him once more and make him hers alone. She could not let that obsession go. She still dreamed that they might somehow be together: only he could put right all that had gone wrong, if only she could win him back. She knew how ill she was and dreamed that he would take her away to some warmer clime where her illness might be cured. He represented her only hope, not just of love, but of life itself. It was when news spread among the farm workers that Lady Stockard was expecting a child of her own that something in Eliza snapped.

"It was Eliza who separated the cream and churned the butter for the house. It was she who filled the milk jugs that were taken up to the Hall each day from the dairy. She knew she had no power left to her but this one. Her obsession for Sir Benjamin still burned desperately in her soul, despite everything – that fierce flame of first love could not be extinguished – but now it entwined poisonously with hate. It enraged her to hear that Lady Stockard was to bear Sir Benjamin's child when her own child had been taken from her. Knowing that her own life was to be cut short by tuberculosis, she decided that they only way for them to be together was to infect Sir Benjamin and drag him after her beyond the veil. Nor would she allow Sir Benjamin's wife to enjoy what had been denied to her. They both had to die."

"But she was discovered?" Mr Corliss rasped.

"Yes. Lady Stockard was the first to become ill even as she carried Sir Benjamin's heir in her womb. More members of the household soon followed as the contagion spread. Eliza had tried her best to hide her illness from the other dairy maids, lest she lose her only way to make a living. But when she caught spitting her diseased sputum into the milk, one of the other maids told Sir Benjamin and as word spread of what she had done, the farm workers gathered in an angry mob. Eliza was seized by Sir Benjamin in front of the gathered crowd and taken into Wakeley Hall. They said she smiled as he took her away – 'Aw I ever wanted wis tae be held in yer airms. This road or the ither, it disnae matter tae me noo. We'll be together in death if no in life. I ken that ye still love me in yer hairt!' That was the last that was ever seen or heard of her.

"Sir Benjamin told everyone that he had spirited her away in the dead of

71

night to protect her from the angry mob and that she was to be sent before the magistrate in another town: as even a creature such as she had a right to a fair trial and justice. Few cared where she was or whether she lived or died, and like as not she would have fallen victim to mob justice had she remained in Wakeley for spreading the pestilence. The outrage of what she done to the family went against every taboo of her station and her sex. And as an outsider, someone from over the border, her crime had fed many old fears and prejudices. People at the Hall and in the village readily accepted Sir Benjamin's side of the story. Only Bonnie knew, or suspected what had really happened to Eliza. Fearing for her own safety, with all that she knew, and the suspicions that now came to rest upon her as another outsider, Bonnie fled in the night and sought shelter here, on Barrow Farm on the outskirts of Thornedale. She kept her own red hair covered, and disappeared among the throng of anonymous farm workers there. In time she married. One of her descendants still lives on Thornedale to this day: Mrs Ellis of Briar Cottage."

Mr Corliss slumped back in his seat, his gaze darting wildly around the fire as he struggled to make sense of all that he had heard.

"I am known for my interest in local tales, and in the private accounts of folk history that seldom make their way into books. It was Mrs Ellis who told me the story herself that had been passed down from Bonnie to her children and grandchildren. Bonnie knew she would not be believed in Wakeley, but she wanted the story to be told, so that someone, even if only the members of her own family, would know what truly happened to Eliza. The family always believed that she was murdered by Sir Benjamin, after he had seduced and abandoned her. Mrs Ellis is a widow and has no children you see. She did not want the story to die with her. All they ever wanted was for someone to know the truth and to believe that Eliza did what she did because she was so cruelly wronged."

"But what she did, Reverend. She blighted them all … "

"Make no mistake, she is far from blameless in the matter. Her actions are unforgiveable, but are we condemn her solely and entirely, as history has done? Are not the actions of Sir Benjamin every bit as wrong and as cruel? For a powerful older man to seduce an innocent and kind-hearted young country girl, to toy with that heart for sport and then abandon Eliza to wait for him endlessly in that blasted ruin of a priory … what chance did she have? Had he not partly murdered her already before he shut her up inside that wall to die so hideously?"

Mr Corliss and Reverend Booth sat in silence for some moments. Mr Corliss scratched his head, unable to clarify his thoughts.

"What she did to him – do you reckon she did it to get her revenge on him or to be with him, you know, in death?"

"Both … " The revered gave a resigned smile. "Is it not strange how often love will not die, sometimes even in the cruelest circumstances?"

Mr Corliss shifted uncomfortably in his seat.

"But Reverend Booth – what of the hairpin with the bee?"

"The Stockard family emblem was the bee. You can still see bees carved into the decorative woodwork at the Hall from the time of the baronets. He would never have given Eliza something so conspicuous as a ring for a token, but some little hairpin – likely one of his wife's that she would not miss. Yes, I see this small item as a very telling one. And to me it speaks of the truth of Bonnie's story: of Sir Benjamin's cruel deception of Eliza and of all his false promises." Reverend Booth sat back in his high-backed armchair and smiled ruefully. "As you may know, Mr Corliss, the bee has often been used in art and mythology as a symbol of resurrection and immortality. How curious then that by your discovery, you have made Eliza Burns and Sir Benjamin live again, in a sense: for do they not live still while we remember them?"

Mr Corliss blanched and drained what little remained in the glass of brandy. All the while Reverend Booth had been talking, one question had burned brighter than all the others in the carpenter's troubled mind. The one question he most wanted to ask – the very problem with which he was most desperately needed the Reverend's help – he simply could not bring himself to voice. The words had come to his lips a dozen times, but he could not speak them, as hard as he tried to summon the courage to do so. Something in the grand bearing of this learned and confident man, speaking so eloquently before him, stayed his tongue each time. *"He will think me mad: a lunatic."*

Thinking with dread of the long drive home that lay ahead of him, and the long dark night that was to follow, Mr Corliss made one last effort to broach the subject, clearing his throat and faltering.

" … Reverend Booth, d-do you believe in … "

The reverend leaned forward, his thick brows furrowing above his gold spectacles as he strained to hear Mr Corliss' hoarse whisper. But the piercing intelligence in the reverend's gaze made the unspeakable word on the tip of Mr Corliss' tongue seem utterly absurd and completely impossible to say out loud.

" … in … the truth of this story?" Mr Corliss prevaricated

The reverend nodded adamantly. "I see no reason to doubt it, Mr Corliss – especially now, with all you have found. Yes, I see your discovery as a complete vindication of the story told by Bonnie Burns of her unfortunate sister. It is proof that Sir Benjamin deceived her with his lies and this false token of love: proof that he murdered her in the most merciless fashion, exactly as Bonnie maintained. It is proof that he is not the blameless and heroic victim in all of this, but rather, the cruel agent of a young woman's destruction, and thereby the destruction of his own family line."

Mr Corliss dropped his head, staring at the rug upon the floor as he inwardly berated himself for his cowardice.

"I hope that may put your mind at rest a little, Mr Corliss. Your discovery was undoubtedly a terrible shock for you, but by this unhappy accident you have exposed a great lie, an historic crime, and a terrible injustice that had been hidden these past two centuries. Wherever the soul of poor Eliza Burns resides now, I am sure that this exposure will give her some peace. It is she for whom I feel most sorry in all of this. For all the great wrong she did, she could never have the one thing she longed for in life, anymore than she can have it now: and what she loved beyond all else destroyed her utterly. I shall pray for her, you may be certain of that."

It was growing dark as Mr Corliss made the long drive back to his cottage from Thornedale. He had lit the little lanterns he kept in the cart for such situations, but was unsure how much oil remained in them since their last use. The exertions of the day had taken a heavy toll and Mr Corliss slumped heavily in his seat – his muffler pulled up high on his face – wishing only to be safely back in the warmth of his bed.

As Peggy walked on steadily before him, he took another swig from the bottle of cough medicine. In the turmoil and confusion of the day he had lost track of when he had been supposed to take the next dose and had resorted to taking a measure of it whenever it felt necessary. Out here in the darkness of the empty back roads, all was silent, save for the rush of low wind that chilled his marrow, and the occasional patter of rain. The cloud hung so heavy in the sky that there were not even any stars to light the way. Mr Corliss strained to think: his mind fatigued beyond endurance.

"What can I do? What can I do? How am I to give her what she wants when the man she wants is dead? And if I cannot? Will she take me instead? I ... another abandoner ... does she seek to punish me for his wrongs? Or for mine? ... But I never

tried to deceive … I never wanted Miss Burrows' love … not hers nor anyone's … I never said I had owt to give to anyone … nor wanted her attentions, even if I did enjoy them at first. Even if I did wonder if I could ever feel that way … "

A low rumble of thunder sounded from the horizon. Mr Corliss shivered, his chin dropping to his chest and his eyelids sore and heavy. He felt his throat itch and he groaned at the thought of what might come when the coughing started again. Out here alone, what might she do to him? He reached for the bottle of cough mixture in his pocket, withdrawing it just as the wheels of the cart jolted over a bump in the road. He felt the bottle slip from his rain-damp fingers and saw the black sheen of its glass dropping, bouncing over the edge of the foot well faster than his weary hand could catch it.

"Nay!"

A sickening smash followed its fall, and Mr Corliss knew at once that there was no point in stopping to see what might be left. The itching in his throat tightened into a twitching spasm that triggered some irresistible reflex to cough that could not be denied.

Mr Corliss marshalled what strength he had left to try to contain the violent impulse shaking his torso: covering his mouth forcefully with his hand against the punishing expulsions of his breath. Another low rumble vibrated through the air, louder this time. His eyes widened as a flash of lightning cracked through the closing darkness and for a second he glimpsed a thin white figure up ahead, standing beside a crooked tree at the left side of the road, its head bowed.

Still he fought to suppress the coughs that felt like they were about to burst through his lungs. He pressed his hand over his mouth more tightly and bent around to his right, his torso convulsing harder as the coughs punched at his lungs with increasing force. Mr Corliss felt a sharp pain and cried out at the feeling of something snapping in his middle back on the left

— instinctively clutching at the pulled muscle with the hand that had been covering his mouth.

Deep choking coughs seized him as they neared the crooked tree. Peggy reared her head and shied to the right as the emaciated white figure appeared again in the flash of lightning and thunder. But as the lightning faded instantly away, the figure did not. As the dreadful coughing went on, pushing Mr Corliss into nausea and dizziness, the ghostly white spectre lingered in his sight, through his tears and through the heavy rain that had begun to fall. As if waiting for them, the figure lifted its head, staring through Mr Corliss with its unblinking and cavernous black sockets. He cried out again at the pain in his back and in his heart, wondering for a moment if his own death might be his only escape. *"But what if she's waiting for me? What if that is what she wants? What if she pursues me even then? Oh God."*

"Oh, Christ! Save me! Help me!" he rasped helplessly up to the thundering heavens above as the coughing at last subsided. He shifted in his seat and cried out again at the searing pain in his back. If he sat perfectly upright and still it was all right, but bending, twisting, and most of all coughing, were now all a matter of acute grief to his strained back.

The thunder and lightning struck again, with all the visceral force of their close proximity overhead, and Mr Corliss could not stop himself from weeping through the rain that coursed down his gaunt face as the familiar white figure was momentarily revealed again a little way further up the lonely road, waiting for the coughing to begin again. And thus continued Mr Corliss' journey home, as the storm, and the coughing, continued to rage on.

.

CHAPTER SEVEN

By the time they reached the drive of his little cottage, one of the lamps of Mr Corliss' cart had sputtered out, and the other offered little assistance as the wind and rain made it very hard to see anything more than a few feet ahead. Mr Corliss struggled to blink the rain from his eyes, trusting Peggy to navigate the familiar way back into the stable through the already open doors. As they began to enter the stable, Peggy suddenly gave a wild neigh, jumping and stamping as her head twisted wildly around. As the suggestion of something spindly and white moving in the darkness at the end of the stable, Mr Corliss leapt from his seat and ran from the stable towards the cottage, satisfied that Peggy was undercover, but unable to do more for her than leave her there as he fled: the pain in his back and the terror in his weary heart rending pitiful whimpers from him as he threw open the back door and burst into the kitchen.

Mr Corliss' raw nerves arrested him in his tracks: made him hold his breath. He could see some dim light through the open door to the hall, he could feel someone in the house: could hear a sound like a footstep creaking on the floor.

"Leave me be, can't you!" he cried wildly, running around the house and throwing open the doors into the little dark rooms of his home. "For the love of God, just leave me be!" He shoved at the door to the parlour and felt his knees buckle under him at the tall dark silhouette of a figure standing before the fire, casting its spindly, dancing shadows upon the wall and the floor.

"Mr Corliss!" Mr Parker exclaimed in alarm, racing forward to catch Mr Corliss' elbow as the blood drained from the carpenter's face and he fell to his knees, dripping and breathless. "Good heavens!"

Mr Corliss could only stare, uncomprehending, into the kindly gentleman's concerned face, as Mr Parker peeled off Mr Corliss' sodden jacket and hat and guided him into his chair by the fire.

"Forgive me, Mr Corliss. I never meant to frighten you – I only came by to see how you were feeling and I got caught in this wretched downpour. I had to leave my horse in your stable. Your back door was open so I thought I would warm myself while I waited for the rain to ease."

Mr Corliss could only stare at him, quite unable to speak. He registered the deep alarm on Mr Parker's features and tried to get himself in hand.

"Whatever were you doing out in this cold, Mr Corliss? I happened to speak to Dr Ronson this afternoon and he mentioned that you were still … rather unwell … "

Mr Corliss screwed tight his eyes as he tried to calm his spasming throat. He swallowed hard. "There was something I had to do," he whispered

He felt Mr Parker's eyes scanning his countenance. *"What did the doctor say to him? Has he come to check if I am losing my mind?"*

"You look dreadfully ill, Mr Corliss, I think I should go and fetch the doctor."

Mr Corliss shook his head, stifling a cry as his pulled muscle caught him painfully again. "Nay," he rasped resolutely. "Nay, thank you, sir," he whispered, trying to soften the fierce intent in his voice and forcing a thin smile. "I shall be fine … only I haven't slept much what with all the coughing."

"Is there something else the matter, Mr Corliss?" Mr Parker knelt down before him, the tender sympathy in the face of his visitor almost undoing Mr Corliss' tightly-clenched composure. "Are you ... troubled still by your discovery of the other day ... ?"

Mr Corliss had to look away, to stare into the coals of the fire as another coughing fit gripped him and he heard with dismay, that second echoey cough grating in time with his own. The sound of his own cough was now something terrible and the urge to vomit at the end of each expulsion of air was almost impossible to resist. He struggled to keep his body still against the violent muscular contractions in his thorax. He struggled not to vomit as Mr Parker stood gaping before him. When he opened his eyes and could breathe again he was horrified at the look at fright in Mr Parker's eyes. Mr Parker was leaning backwards and covering his mouth: his cheeks blanched.

"Oh, Mr Corliss ... I ... I ... How can I help you?" he whispered earnestly.

"Nowt but a cough," Mr Corliss shook his head, "and my back is strained from all the exertion. I shall be fine ... "

The two men exchanged a long glance, Mr Corliss hoping that the pain and terror he felt would not show in his blood-shot eyes as Mr Parker's searching gaze held him.

"Nothing else troubles you?"

Mr Corliss looked away and shook his head.

"Very well. I also wished to let you know that the ... body has been returned to the village. There is to be a burial service at the church this Saturday at two, to which you are of course invited, should you be well enough, or ... wish to attend."

Mr Corliss sat up very straight in his chair, some thought occurring to him at the news.

"Where … " Mr Corliss hesitated, careful to try to conceal the intensity of his interest. "Where is the burial to be?"

"Ah, in the unconsecrated section of the churchyard, I believe, as we do not know for certain the young woman's name, or her faith. Still, Mrs Astley has arranged for a proper casket and so on. Ah, Mr Parsons is taking care of everything I understand. The young woman will be laid to rest properly, Mr Corliss." Mr Parker nodded reassuringly, something unreadable in his eyes that Mr Corliss worried was suspicion about his sanity. "Reverend Vine will perform the service. I hope you can take some comfort in that. Your discovery will allow this poor woman to be laid to rest at last, to have the proper burial that every Christian deserves. I hope that will … help you … in dealing with all of this … "

Mr Corliss could say nothing for fear of starting the coughing again. He simply nodded and stared back into the coals, some serious momentous idea formulating in his mind.

"Well, if you are certain you do not wish the doctor, I shall say goodnight, Mr Corliss. I shan't expect you back at work for the time being. I can see that you are quite unwell. Perhaps you will permit me to call by again?"

Mr Corliss nodded absently, his eyes narrowing as he stared into the coals, his numb hands unconsciously drawing the rug on the chair around his shoulders. He did not hear Mr Parker closing the door as he left the house, nor the whinnying of Mr Parker's white stallion, Bobby, as he manoeuvred him around Peggy and the hastily parked cart and out of the stable. He tried very hard to think clearly, to follow the train of thought that Mr Parker's news had suggested to him. *"Perhaps a proper burial will lay her to rest? Nay, but that is never what she wants — she only wants 'him.' Oh Lord, tell me, what am I to do? I'm sure Mr Parker thinks me insane. If only I could rest, just for a while. I'm so tired and I feel so ill. I've never felt so alone … "*

Something in what Mr Parker had said had given him a tiny seed of hope – some notion that had flashed through his tortured mind. But as he slumped in the chair, exhausted and in pain, his thoughts circling and spinning, tumbled away from him. In only a few moments, and despite his desperate determination to retrieve that tiny lost hope from the depths of his mind, he was asleep.

Through fragmented and restless dreams he moaned and wheezed, his clammy fingers twitching in his lap as if trying to shoo something away. He felt cold hands on his waxy face, as if someone stood behind him with thin fingers splayed out and resting on his temples and down to the hinge of his jaw. At times in his life he had longed for just such a gentle touch as this, but while a part of his dreaming mind welcomed the unfamiliar contact, some life-long instinct stirred at the danger it registered, and the pulse in Mr Corliss' sinewy neck quickened.

His head twitched a little from side to side as his dreaming self were trying to shake the fingers away. He felt them slide slowly down his face with a sensation at once tantalising, as the feathery touch reached his neck, and alarming for the suggestion of sharp points on the nails or fingers that his skin registered. He groaned again, whimpering as the fingers encircled his throat and began to squeeze. He could feel something blocking his throat, something in his throat, choking him from the inside, even as the fingers choked him from the outside. He couldn't breathe and began to cough and gasp hopelessly for air.

Mr Corliss' eyes opened in panic and confusion, trying to breathe as something gripped his throat and something else blocked his airway. Instinct threw him forwards, his desperate attempts to cough propelling something to shoot out from his drawn and pale lips. It trailed in a short arc to the carpet, something gleaming metallic in the firelight with a wispy tail behind it. He gasped again, jolting himself out of the chair with a cry as the feeling of hands around his throat dissolved into the night air. He span around: one hand at his throat and the other clutching at the sharp pain in his back. No-one was there. Yet still on the sides of his face and around his neck he felt the terrible sensation where the phantom fingers had touched him, where they had choked him.

He coughed and pawed at his wet mouth, his fingers raking his tongue at the suggestion of some foreign wiry object that should not be there. His fingers caught something and pulled at it, drawing it out: a single hair, very long, curling and shining a coppery orange in the firelight. He turned back to where the object he had coughed out had fallen: a sickening feeling sinking heavily in the pit of his stomach. There on the hearthrug lay the uncoiled tress of red curling hair, affixed to an antique silver pin ornamented with a stylised bee. Mr Corliss knelt carefully, stiffly, constrained by the pain in his back, and picked it up. Catching his breath and shivering in his still wet clothes, he held the tress and pin gingerly between the tips of his thumb and forefinger, turning them in the light as he recognised all the details he remembered from when he held them before.

He gave a violent shudder and placed the item onto the mantel. His hand gripped the ledge of the mantelpiece and he leaned on it heavily, his head bent down towards the fire. "*She can touch things, move things now. She can touch me, hurt me. Aye, her strength is growing even as mine fails. She is draining the life and strength from my body, even from my mind. How can this end but in …* " He shuddered again, shaking the thought from his mind. "*It can't be — none of this can be,*" some more rational part of his mind reasoned. "*You are sick, delirious. You must be imagining it all.*" He gazed up at the pin and lock of hair resting on the mantel, knowing beyond doubt that he had not retrieved them from their hiding place. He had not even given them a thought since he had put them there — how long ago had it been? Only a few days? It seemed like an eternity.

"But if I am not imagining it ... ?" he demanded hoarsely to the empty room. On the skin of his face and neck the uneasy feeling of a stranger's touch still lingered. He shook his head, trying to dislodge the sensory after-image but it lingered still. He lit a candle from the fire and raced to his darkened bedroom, hurtling breathlessly towards the mirror above the wash-stand.

A rasping whimper escaped his lips as he turned his face this way and that. White marks, the impressions of slender, icy fingers, dotted the sides of his face from them temple to the hinges of the jaw. His throat tickled painfully as he narrowed his eyes in pain and raised his chin. His throat was ringed with the same white marks, as if long skeletal fingers had pressed and squeezed there. He shook his head more vehemently. He knew he had not made the marks himself: beyond the fact that his hands were broad, his fingers much larger than the marks suggested, he could never have positioned his hands to make such impression upon his own face and neck.

"She touched me ... touched me!"

The anguish in his voice spasmed into a cough, and he braced himself with both hands upon the sides of the wash-stand as the fit took hold: turning his head for fear of his cough extinguishing the candle and leaving him in the dark as the echoes of a second cough began to sound in time with his own. He screwed shut his eyes as something misty began to coalesce in the darkness behind him in the mirror's reflection.

"Leave me be. Please, just leave me be!"

He tried to keep still as the coughing wrenched sharply at the pulled muscle in his back: tried to contain the violence of the coughs. Something brushed the sides of his neck, as insubstantial and as unbearable as the touch of a spider's web. The coughs deepened into guttural barking, squeezing all the air from his lungs, grinding membrane to membrane in sickening, dizzying convulsions. Mr Corliss could not move with the effort of trying to stay upright, trying not to vomit or lose consciousness as the coughing fit continued. Something encircled his neck, cold, bony and tightening. Tears streamed from his closed eyes – he could not bring himself to open them. The thought of seeing what was happening seemed even more insupportable than feeling it. For a moment he wondered if he should not simply let her have her way. But the idea of being forced to go with her beyond the grave, wherever she wished to take him held more horror than the thought of merely dying. The feeling of being trapped with someone who wished only to hurt him burst open some long boarded-up door in his memory, as his knees began to buckle from the lack of oxygen flowing to his brain.

"What do you want? What do you want!" he cried in breathless wheezing gasps as the coughing and the choking phantom fingers dropped him to the cold and dusty floor. Involuntarily, he curled into a ball facing the wall, just as he had so often done as a child, trying to clench his whole body as small as possible and trying to will himself through the wall. The feeling of fingers around his neck seemed to loosen and a breath of icy air touched his ear as a breathless whisper rose above the sounds of the wind and rain outside.

" … Him … Him … "

Mr Corliss suddenly ceased to tremble. He simply nodded. All at once, he understood. That faint spark of hope he had thought he had just glimpsed during Mr Parker's visit now caught flame in the blackness of his mind.

"I can help you … I will help you … "

It was a quarter to three in the morning as Mr Corliss drove the cart down the dark back roads towards the village, quietly urging the sleepy

Peggy onwards. He had hurriedly changed out of his wet clothes, and now, rugged up and protected by his waterproof oilskin coat, wearing a dark broad brimmed hat and with a woollen muffler covering his neck and face, only his bloodshot but fiercely resolved eyes showed in the darkness of the wet and windy night.

Fortified by several swigs from the dusty bottle of old cough medicine that he had found again in the kitchen, Mr Corliss felt for the first time in days that a wisp of hope might be within his grasp. The fear of what he intended to do struck him, but weighed against the fear of what would happen were he to do nothing, it seemed by far the lesser of two evils. In the back of the cart he had put some blankets, a dark lantern, and a hessian sack packed with rags wrapped around some off-cuts of wood from his workshop. He changed the reins into his left hand to feel with his right in his pockets for the items he had stored there.

The wind rose again and Mr Corliss was glad of it. At least it might mask the sound of his cart, of any noise he might make in his nocturnal endeavours. No lights shone in the sparsely scattered houses on the outskirts of Wakeley. He stiffened himself upright in his seat, painfully aware of the soreness in his back and of the tiredness he must fight against. *"I must do this … for if I don't … I must help her … help her as I could not help my mother … I must … "*

At length he pulled the reins and Peggy's sluggish walk came to a stop. He steeled himself with another swig from the medicine bottle and climbed carefully down from the cart. All was dark and still in the cottage up ahead. He swallowed painfully and walked around the cart, gently lifting out the hessian sack and lighting the dark lantern, closing the cover so only a sliver of candlelight shone out. He threw one of the blankets over his shoulder and took up the lantern.

Mr Corliss crept forwards in the darkness, reminding himself of the numerous times he had come to this place in daylight and going over the layout of the premises in his mind. Mr Parsons had sometimes ordered caskets from him when his regular supplier out of town was too busy to fill his meagre orders. He had never liked making coffins, but now he was glad that he had.

Mr and Mrs Parsons kept the post office in Wakeley, and being of an enterprising turn of mind, Mr Parsons had long ago realised that the one thing missing in Wakeley was an undertaker's, and that if he, well known to everyone in the village, should add this service to those he already offered, he would not only be providing a great service to the community, but he would be saving his friends and neighbours from having to give their custom, and their money, to the longer-established undertaking firm of Morris and Sons in Thornedale.

In the interests of keeping his overheads low and his profits high, Mr Parsons had only had to extend his cottage a little with the addition of a mortuary and a viewing parlour at the side of the building. For what small but regular demand there was for his services in Wakeley, it had proved quite sufficient. Mrs Parsons' initial squeamishness in the matter had been assuaged by the gradual realisation that her friends and neighbours could do her no harm when their time came to pay her one final visit on their way to Wakeley's churchyard cemetery. The notion that every member of the Wakeley community would one day also have to pay a modest but not inconsiderable sum of money to her and her husband, further eased her discomfort on the subject of the mortuary at the side of her home.

Mr Corliss crept towards the side door of the cottage, where in days past he had come in daylight to deliver the occasional casket. It was a subject of some pride in Wakeley that no-one bothered to lock their doors, and that no-one ever needed to. Mr Corliss hoped that this was true of the Parsons tonight. He held his breath as he tried the doorknob, ever so gently. A wave of relief washed over him as he felt it turn and he lifted the door as he opened it just a little, his ear straining to detect whether it creaked or not as the wind continued to whistle and the rain to patter on the slate roof.

He thought for a moment as he hesitated by the door, and he slipped out of his boots, lest he leave a trail of water and mud upon the floor to betray his visit. His dripping coat he hung upon a branch of the spindly tree close to the door. With his dark lantern in one hand and his hessian sack in the other, he paused. *"What am I doing? Can I really do such a thing? What if I am caught? Whatever could I say? I could never explain. I will be locked up for a burglar, if not for a madman!"*

But the thought of her touch – the unbearable notion that she might touch him again - impelled him over the threshold. To be trapped with someone whom he could not escape, someone whose touch he could not elude, who might harm him: he simply could not submit to such a thing again. *"I would sooner go to jail or the madhouse if it comes to that. I have to try. I must escape her, set her free."*

Mr Corliss listened intently as he lingered inside the doorway: he could hear nothing but the sound of the storm outside. *"You must go on. You must do it."* He nodded sombrely to himself, shifting the weight of the sack and trying not to cry out at the pain in his back that it caused him. He tiptoed through the immaculate parlour where Mr Parsons greeted his customers. Viewings were sometimes arranged at the far end of the rectangular room, where a platform rested surrounded by Mrs Parsons' artfully draped curtains, and two tall vases of flowers. *"This time tomorrow it will be only a memory, a nightmare to be forgotten. I know you are desperately afraid but you must go on. You have no choice."*

Mr Corliss halted at the curtained doorway that divided the parlour from the mortuary behind it. It had discomforted him to visit such a place in daylight, but now ... his skin prickled at the thought of his task. He strained to listen again for any sounds from the house beyond, but could hear nothing. He drew aside the curtain a little way and shone the dark lantern into the room. There on the metal table in the centre of the room rested a plain closed casket. He drew in his breath and tried to calm his thoughts. Scanning the rest of the room he saw only the implements of Mr Parsons' business, and the various bottles of fluid and jars of emollients and chemicals he used upon the dead. She would need no such care – she would receive no such ministrations. Already preserved, mummified in her fashion, she waited only for the grave and the priest's words.

Mr Corliss sighed at the thought and opened the shade of the dark lantern a little wider, stepping into the room and setting down his hessian sack carefully upon the floor. Next, he set the lantern on one of the benches at the side of the room and took the folded blanket from his shoulder, spreading it out upon the floor. Drawing a screwdriver from his pocket, he gently positioned it into one of the screws on the lid of the casket and began his work. In a minute or two he had removed all six screws securing the lid and dropped them into his pocket.

He braced himself to lift the lid – not against the weight of the cheap casket, as the wood was flimsy and light in his strong hands, but against the sight of her. *"Her body can't hurt you … it can't …it's dead … just dead bones …"* Yet to see her again, as he moved the lid aside, struck him with the same visceral impact as his first sight of her through the cloud of dust that had billowed from the broken brick wall of the cellar. He was stung again with a sense of fear, anger, pain and helplessness all swirled together into one choking mass.

She had been placed on her right side to fit into the casket: her curled up legs unable to be released, nor her bound arms untied from their centuries-old bonds. She held her position – the position Sir Benjamin had placed her in – just as she still held onto her obsession, her grudge; her tormented love that was still bound insolubly with hate. At the sight of her open mouth beneath the hands covering her eyes, Mr Corliss' throat convulsed and his lungs felt the punch of his lungs forcefully compressing. He tried to stifle the cry in his throat and the coughs that fought to burst from his tightly-pursed lips, his body jerking forward involuntarily and with it the casket lid clutched in his hands. He could see the lid of the casket catching the dark lantern on the edge of the bench but could do nothing to stop it. The crash of the metal lantern hitting the hard floor in this unfurnished room would surely reverberate through the house to the Parsons' bedroom, even above the sound of the wind.

Mr Corliss lurched forward, gritting his teeth against the flash of pain in his back as he reached out desperately for the lantern, his finger catching the narrow metal loop of its handle only inches from the floor. He stifled his coughs into the crook of his arm then paused to catch his breath. Gingerly he rested the casket lid up against a bare patch of wall between two benches, making sure it would not fall. He turned back to the casket holding up the dark lantern over the curled up figure bound by centuries of restless unrequited love and torment within.

A tear came to his eyes to see her again. She was so small, so withered. He set the lantern down again a little way back from the edge of the bench.

"Forgive me, Miss Eliza," he whispered as he reached into the casket, unsure, not wanting to touch her, but knowing that he must. He reached under the bent knees and hunched shoulders, wincing at the terrible hardness of the desiccated flesh and barely covered bones. He felt a breath of cold air sigh behind his left ear as he lifted her, at arm's length, out of the casket and set her down on the blanket he had placed upon the floor. She weighed so little, no more than a sack of rags and scraps of wood.

Quickly now he took up the hessian sack and placed it into the casket, just where she had lain. With all the speed he could muster, Mr Corliss set to replacing and tightening each screw in the casket lid, mindful, all the while, of the figure crouched at his feet in the gloom: unwilling to look at her and desperate to take her away. Behind the sound of the wind he could not be sure, but more than once he held his breath at the suggestion of a whistling sigh, a wheezing breath that seemed each time to further chill the air in the darkened mortuary. He worried that behind his back the figure might have found the strength to stand, to stretch its crumbling and brittle limbs. He half-expected to feel its bony fingers on his shoulder, at his throat: more than once he turned around, not enough to look upon her fully, but just enough to see that she remained, unmoving, where he had put her. There was little enough comfort in that.

Mr Corliss made a quick check that his tools were back in his pockets, swept away some dust that had dropped from the hessian sack onto the floor. All was as it had been save for her, crouching on the blanket on floor. Gathering up the blanket around her, he picked her up, hooking the dark lantern over one of his fingers before carefully navigating his way through the door curtain, out through the stillness of the parlour and through the outer door into the wind and rain of the night. He closed the door quietly behind him.

He stepped back into his boots and pulled his oilskin roughly over his head and shoulders as he carried his burden back to the cart, trying all the while not to think of her, not to look at her, not to breathe in the charnel house smell of her, nor to imagine that the cold air that sometimes puffed at his left ear and chilled his hollow cheek was anything but the natural motions of the night wind.

Mr Corliss set Eliza's body down in the back of the cart and covered it with another blanket. He looked back over his shoulder at the Parsons' house in the distance – relieved to see no lights in their windows: nothing to disturb the oblivion of their sleep.

Gently rousing Peggy from her dozing, Mr Corliss climbed back into the cart and slowly set off once more as the wind and rain intensified. How strange and unfamiliar the landscape seemed in the pitch black of night; how strange and unfamiliar to himself he felt to be abroad at such a time and doing such foul business as this. As the cart rolled on past the last houses and turned off into a back road, Mr Corliss could not help but look back at the black shape under a blanket behind him. It seemed utterly impossible that he could have done such a thing. To have stolen a dead body: perhaps he was going mad after all. He frowned to think of the desperate state he had reached, and wondered if even this plan he had fashioned, as bizarre and outlandish as he knew it was, would bring an end this madness that had entangled him.

Wearily he felt himself begin to cough again and he tried to brace himself to spare his back the inevitable pain the exertion would bring. Something made him turn his head to the tray of the cart, and his face twisted in pain at the suggestion of a misty white shape around the blanketed figure, as if the poor unquiet spirit was trying vainly to reinhabit its long broken body. He could not look for more than a instant. He tried to tell himself that it was only mist in the cold night air. He urged Peggy onwards into the night.

It was not long before they reached their destination. Mr Corliss pulled up the cart under the shelter of a large tree and climbed down. He looked around nervously, half-expecting to see someone watching him, in spite of the hour and the darkness. Downing another swig of the cough mixture, he tried to steady his resolve.

"Breaking into an undertaker's was one thing, but this? Surely it is a terrible sacrilege? How can it be anything other than wrong? What if God punishes me for it? But could that be any worse that what I have thus far endured? Where was God to help me these last endless days and nights? Where was He to help Eliza when she was

bricked up in that wall? Where was He to help my mother? Perhaps all of this has been my punishment for not helping her myself, and this act shall be my salvation?"

The wind rose sharply, sending a violent shiver through the trees. Peggy reared her head and Mr Corliss shuddered.

"Right or wrong, I can't see any other way out of this. Whether I be damned or not, I have no choice if I am to try to free myself from her, and to free her from her torment. Am I any better than her – doing wrong because I can see no other way: because I am desperate and afraid and alone? We are both lost souls, alone ... "

Picking up a long cloth-wrapped article from the cart and hanging the dark lantern from one finger, Mr Corliss took a deep breath and scooped up the blanket-shrouded figure in his arms. With dread in his heart he crossed the road and approached the door of the St Elizabeth's church.

"This is all I have ... all I have left to try ... if this doesn't work, I don't know what I shall do ... but how can it work? It is madness ... "

Trying to ignore the voice of rising panic in his head, Mr Corliss looked out across the churchyard cemetery behind the church and strained to make out the row of tall trees beyond the field that masked the vicarage in its grounds that were bounded by the river on the other side. All he could see was blackness. He hoped that the trees would hide any light that might be visible through the stained glass of the church. He hoped most of all that the vicar, Reverend Vine, was not awake to witness the desecration of his beloved church. Mr Corliss' eyes scanned all around once more before he held his breath and pushed open the door.

Treading carefully, afraid of bumping into statues or tripping over the legs of tables bearing vases of flowers, lest he break anything or drop what he was carrying, Mr Corliss tried to focus all his attention onto the narrow beam of light that shone from the partially opened gate of the dark lantern. Moving hesitantly through the vestibule, his footsteps echoing conspicuously, Mr Corliss entered the nave, feeling for a moment as though

he were walking down the aisle with a bride to give away. *"And so I am …*
with a dead bride for a dead bridegroom … "

On he processed along the centre aisle, his eyes sweeping around the
empty pews, the high glass windows, and down to the stones under his feet.
He gave a cough, cringing as it echoed up into the high vaulted void, and
stiffening as he heard another cough echo behind him. Quickening his pace,
he breasted the front-most row of pews and hesitated as he reached the
arched chancel that housed the raised altar with its great glass window
behind. Unsure of what else to do, Mr Corliss set down the shrouded body
upon the raised platform of the altar and opened the dark lantern to its
brightest light.

Of course he had seen the old ledger stones in the floor of the chancel
before, but had never taken much notice of them beyond the fact that they
were there and that they were old. With the lantern in his hand he crouched
down to better read the inscriptions upon the cracked and time-worn
stones. Beginning at the far left side of the chancel he skimmed over the
hard to read antique script of the carvings until he saw the name "Sir Roger
Stockard, Baronet. Also his wife, Lady Margaret Stockard," with their
respective dates of birth and death. The next two stones recorded the
names of "Sir Matthew Stockard" and "Lady Patience Stockard," and
several short-lived children. To the right of these stones another ledger
stone in carved black marble, cracked diagonally at the bottom, caught Mr
Corliss' eye. Something about it was a little grander than its neighbours.
Being slightly out of the most central path of foot traffic to the altar, it was
somewhat less worn than the stones in the middle. It bore a carved coat of
arms: a shield, with three bees over a field intersected by three vertical lines.
Mr Corliss traced the words over with his finger.

"Here lyeth interred the body of Sir Benjamin Stockard, Baronet, eldest
son of Sir Matthew Stockard, who died December 18th, An. Dom. 1744,

Aged 41 years.

Also Lady Anne his wife, the youngest daughter of Sir Peter Garrard, who died May 5th, An. Dom. 1743, aged 26 years.

Also their son, Matthew Roger Stockard, who died, January 8th, An. Dom. 1743, aged 7 months.

In God's Hands."

Mr Corliss unwrapped the long implement had brought in with him from the cart and crouched there, above the ledger stone holding the icy crowbar in his hands. Looking at the size of the stone he wondered if he could move it at all. And what if it cracked more than it already had? If he damaged the stone it would be obvious something had happened – he might be discovered.

His fingers traced around the edges of the stone, where it fitted neatly and flush with the other floor stones. There was no gap, no space large enough for the crowbar to find some purchase. There was only the crack to try. It ran from side to side in a diagonal line in the lower third of the stone. Its edges were already a little ragged.

Focussing all of his attention onto this mechanical problem, the sort of problem he was used to dealing with every day when he worked, Mr Corliss tried to put from his mind the reasons why he was in the church and the silent witness who was watching him from the altar. As delicately as he could, he insinuated the fine flat edge of the bar between the two cracked segments of the black ledger stone and gently moved the lever. The shorter segment of the stone shifted slightly, only a little, but enough for Mr Corliss to work the flat of the bar further down into the narrow gap.

In a minute or two, through all the skill earned over his long years at his trade, and by the strenuous exertions of his strong arms and powerful grasp, he had managed to lever up the smaller section of the stone. He had wedged the crowbar's wrapping cloth underneath the bar, to protect the longer segment of stone from downward force of the lever. Now he grasped the raised up edge of smaller section in his hands and with a cry of pain he dragged and swung it up, until it rested on the lip of the vault if had covered. Mr Corliss straightened up, clutching his back where the pain scorched his nerves. He sat down and pushed at the raised stone with all the strength of his legs and feet until it slid back.

He was not sure what he expected to see in the brick vault below the ledger stone. He had half-thought it would be a mess of dirt and bits of bone. But he could see, now that the lower third of the vault was exposed, that a casket lay there, apparently intact, although it seemed to be tilted a little to one side. The lid of the casket lay about one to two feet down below the top of the vault, as though perhaps leaving room for another casket on top, or …

"What if they are all enclosed in the one coffin? No, please no … she would not want that … "

Mr Corliss' heart sank at the thought, and he grabbed at the dark lantern, lowering it down into the vault to try to see if anything lay beneath the casket before his eyes. His eyes narrowed. Yes. Yes, down below the bottom of the casket there were fragments, pieces of wood, of some other earlier casket, and the suggestion of a piece of bone.

"Of course," he tried to calm his panic, *"the wife and child died before him, and they would have been interred before him. And a man of his status would warrant his own casket … a man like that … an arrogant, heartless man who cared for nothing but himself, who thought so little of his wife as to … "*

Mr Corliss clenched his jaw, a surge of strange energy lending power to his arm as he grabbed the crowbar and forced it under the bottom edge of the larger segment of the ledger stone, bracing the bar against the rim of the brick vault and forcing it down with a brisk exhalation of air.

"Kill her, will you?" he heard himself cry out loud, the hot sting of tears welling in his eyes. "Murder her, will you!" he exclaimed hoarsely as the stone rose and he began to push at it fiercely with his boots, bumping it, nudging it, little by little until its edge balanced on the rim of stones around the vault. He crouched low over the raised stone, no longer feeling the sharp pain is his back as he gripped the cracked edge of the stone in fists clenched white. "You thought yourself so clever!" he hissed with a jerk of the stone that sent it grating back a few inches to the side of the vault. "You thought yourself so powerful to use a woman so ill who only wanted to love you!" The stone slid again under the fierce power of his rage. "You thought she counted for nowt!" The stone moved further to the side. "You thought yours was the power to decide her life or death – to blight her life with your hate! You had no right! You had no right to treat her so cruelly! You had no right to destroy her!"

Mr Corliss fell back with a deep sigh as the stone shifted clear of the vault. He wiped at the tears coursing down his red cheeks and wiped roughly at his running nose with his sleeve. Getting to his feet, he stood at the foot of the vault, staring down hard on the fragile wooden casket below him. Through the caked dust he could make out a tarnished silver coffin plate affixed to the casket's lid. The name was large and plain enough, even through the dust: Sir Benjamin Stockard.

Down on his knees, Mr Corliss reached into the vault and pulled at the casket lid, feeling it yield to his strength, as rusted nails slid easily from the dried and shrunken planks of the casket. He set the unstable lid upside down upon the large segment of stone and looked down upon the mortal remains of Sir Benjamin. The skeleton appeared mostly intact, its dust-encrusted and sepia coloured bones lying in a carpet of dirt and fragments of rotted tissue and cloth. In the light of the lantern, two golden rings shone on the skeletal fingers. The skull was tilted over to the right, as if trying to look over its shoulder towards the figure some feet above and behind it by the altar.

A sob burst from Mr Corliss and tears he could no longer contain coursed down his gaunt face. He was not aware that he was clutching the crowbar tightly in his right hand, nor did he care if anyone could hear him now as he yelled at the skeleton with all the ferocity that was left in his aching and torn voice. "I could not stop you then. I could not protect her from you. But here I am now, and here she is, returned to claim what she desires!" Mr Corliss arm swooped the crowbar over his head and down to smash the grinning skull below his feet. "There! How do you like it?" he wept through gritted teeth. "How do you like some of your own medicine? You had no right! You had no right! How do you like that? It is the least you deserve. The least I can do to repay you."

Mr Corliss looked at the crowbar in his hand and dropped it with a clang to the floor. Sniffing and wiping roughly at his still streaming face, he dropped down to his knees, reaching into the disturbed casket to roughly pull one of the gold rings off Sir Benjamin's finger bone. He did not cringe as the bone fell out of the ring he snatched up. He no longer feared. Blind with rage he stalked to the altar and took up the body of Eliza in his arms, unable to stifle his weeping as he carried her back to the brick vault.

"Now, Sir Benjamin, your bride has come to claim you," he hissed through his tears. "Here, before God at the altar of your church, the woman who loved you – the one you abandoned and destroyed has returned to you, to be joined with you, forever!"

Mr Corliss lowered the stiff body down into the vault, setting her down on her side over the chest of the skeleton with a sickening crunch of brittle bone and rotten wood beneath her weight. He placed Sir Benjamin's ring upon her ring finger.

"Now at last he is yours, as you wished," he growled. "Never to be parted again." Angrily he fished in his breast pocket, drawing out in his damp fingers the silver bee hairpin and its coiled tress of red hair.

"There!" He held it out towards the pitiful figure curled up on the skeleton below him. "There," he whispered, sadly and more quietly, feeling all the rage and hate draining from his body. Gently he reached into the vault and placed the hairpin to rest on Eliza's head. He sighed, his tears easing. "There … you have what you wanted at last. He is yours now, as he promised you. Now, Eliza Burns, I pray you let me be forevermore."

Mr Corliss's shoulders hunched as he felt again the familiar aching twitch in the back of his burning throat. The first cough punched the air from his lungs and he gasped for air, barking again and again as dizziness and nausea doubled him over. Something was blocking his throat, something in his airway choking him so that he coughed harder desperate to clear it at last. With painful, breathless force, and the sound of a choking animal, he half coughed, half vomited a mouthful of some foul black sticky, hairy matter into the grave, over the feet of the skeleton of Sir Benjamin Stockard.

He whimpered as the coughing ceased. He wiped his mouth on his sleeve, wiped his face with his hands. It was done. All that remained was to replace the ledger stone and leave.

No-one in Wakeley Hall heard the crash that night. No-one woke to the sound. It was not until the next morning that one of the house-maids up early to light the fires discovered the large painting that had fallen from the wall during the early hours of the morning. No-one thought it odd that such a heavy old frame should give way after hanging so long in its place the wall, presiding over the top of the grand carved oak staircase of the Hall. Mrs Astley found it merely inconvenient to have to send the large 18th century portrait of Sir Benjamin Stockard away to have its frame repaired.

Mr Corliss closed the kitchen door behind him. Peggy had been unharnessed and had fallen asleep almost before he had finished in the stable. Sleep … Mr Corliss could barely remember how it felt to sleep. Every fibre, every bone in him ached. It had taken all his strength to replace the ledger stone over the brick vault, but he had done it. He had checked over his tracks, making sure to leave not a hair, not a speck to betray what he had done. Yes, he had done just what he had meant to do. But would it be enough? Now he was past caring.

He had dosed himself with the cough medicine when he got back to the cart, doing his best with raw and shaking hands not to spill it, nor to drop it. The drive back to his cottage in the rainy darkness of early morning had been a blur. He felt numb, different somehow … but he had been forced to *be* different. What did that signify? *"Oh, I can't think any more … "*

It was after five in the morning. He was lucky that he had not been seen by any of the local farmers. *"Or if I was, it was too dark and rainy for them to recognise me … "* He trudged to his bedroom, using the dark lantern in preference to the trouble of lighting another candle. His feet dragged heavily on the hall carpet. He cast off his wet clothes and threw them weakly towards the wooden chair in the corner of his room. The fire was out and he could not summon the strength even to relight it.

He set the old bottle of cough medicine down on the bedside table and fell into his bed in his underclothes, pulling up the covers as high as his sore arms would allow. The blankets seemed as heavy as lead. He sank into the pillow, closed his eyes and slept.

CHAPTER EIGHT

There was a knocking. Some distant sound of knocking that drew Mr Corliss up from the depths of his slumber. He opened his eyes, not sure what time, what day it might be. Someone was knocking on his front door: that much his fogged mind could determine.

He pulled himself out of bed, painfully aware of the strained muscles in his back, arms and legs. Even his hands, the joints of his fingers ached as he pulled on the dressing gown that hung ever on a hook at the back of his bedroom door.

"Just a minute," he muttered, more to himself than whoever was knocking. He rubbed at his eyes, wondering why they felt so swollen as he shuffled down the hall towards the door. Images from the night before flooded back into his mind in a torrent that set his pulse racing. Had someone discovered what he had done? Had he been seen after all? Had they come for him now?

No longer caring what might happen, he sighed and opened the unlocked door, startled to see not the police but the friendly, concerned face of Mr Parker standing before him in the glaring light.

"Oh," he rasped, "Hello, Mr Parker?"

"Oh, did I wake you, Mr Corliss? I'm terribly sorry, only I merely wished to see how are feeling today."

Mr Corliss rubbed his head, sleepily, feeling profoundly confused. "Ah, what time is it, please?"

Mr Parker smiled, checking the time from his gold pocket watch. "I make it four thirty, Mr Corliss. I had intended to call by earlier but all these problems we've been having in the dairy with the milk of late have taking up more time that I had intended. How is that cough of yours today?"

Mr Corliss paused. He had slept since five in the morning – nearly twelve hours solid – and he could not recall waking even once to cough. Even now, although his throat was sore, rough, raw even, that itching, that tickling spasm seemed to be gone at last. He took a deep breath, and even in spite of the pain that persisted in his pulled back muscle, a wave of relief washed over him. He could breathe freely at last.

"I reckon it's a sight better," he said cautiously. "I've slept today better than I have in … " Mr Corliss trailed off, smiling to himself, then to Mr Parker. "Aye, I do feel better."

"I'm very glad to hear it." Mr Parker smiled back. "I also wished to remind you about the service tomorrow for, ah, the young lady's remains. I don't know if you wish to come or … ?"

"Aye," Mr Corliss stated firmly. "Aye, I should like that very much."

"Well, that's splendid, Mr Corliss. I'm very pleased. And I know that Mrs Astley will be very glad to see you there also. Ah, is there anything I can get for you? Anything you need at the moment?"

Mr Corliss politely shook his head. "Nay, I'm grand, thank you."

"Well, that's splendid, Mr Corliss. I shall look forward to seeing you tomorrow then, around two at St Elisabeth's. Good day now."

"'Day to you," Mr Corliss croaked, unable to keep the suggestion of a smile from his lips.

It was nearing the hour of two the next day as Mr Corliss hastened Peggy towards the church. After Mr Parker's visit he had paused only for a cup of tea and a piece of bread and butter before returning to bed. Sleep, profound and restful had held him in its soothing embrace until he had woken after midday the next day and realised that he must hurry to bathe, shave, and find some decent clothes to wear before hastening to try to get to churchyard in time for the service.

He felt a pang of nervousness as he pulled up his cart under the same tree that had sheltered him the last time he had come here under cover of darkness. Had it really happened? In the light of day, it seemed impossible, unreal. And yet his fingers still bore the scratches of the black marble ledger stone's sharp edges. His knuckles still bore the bruises of its crushing weight. He felt the grim reality of that night in his still aching arms and legs. He could only hope and pray that his act remained undiscovered: that Mr Parsons, the undertaker, would have no reason to look inside the sealed casket of the long-deceased and nameless woman in his charge, and that Reverend Vine had not detected anything amiss in his beloved church.

Mr Corliss gave Peggy a gentle pat to reassure himself as much as her, before he crossed the road and approached the church. As he rounded the doorway of the church and came in view of the churchyard behind him, he caught his breath and stopped dead in his tracks.

There in the distance, visible through the tombstones of the churchyard and dwarfed by the line of tall trees beyond that swayed slightly in the cool breeze stood a figure, small and slight, with her back toward him: her hair red, and piled upon her head. The shape of the figure seemed so impossibly familiar – so impossible that he had to grasp the stone wall of the church wall for support as he caught his breath.

The figure looked down at the ground, head bowed in that familiar posture, still and silent until it suddenly turned towards him, not seeing him, but looking at something else behind the church with a pleasant and mild face of a milky-white complexion. The woman replaced her hat on her head and walked towards whatever she had been looking at, smiling, and mouthing words that Mr Corliss could not hear from where he stood.

Something crunched on the gravel path behind him and Mr Corliss spun around to see Mr Parker walking towards him.

"Afternoon, Mr Corliss, I'm very glad to see you looking so much better today."

"How do," Mr Corliss replied, his voice still hoarse, but stronger than before.

"Shall we join the others? I think it must be almost time, if you are ready." Mr Parker gestured for Mr Corliss to step onto the path that led around the side of the church and back to the grassy churchyard beyond, where grey and lichened tombstones marked the resting places of villagers gone before.

"Ah, others?" Mr Corliss enquired nervously as they walked among the stones, noting the little group of people standing some way distant in the field between the churchyard and the row of tall trees beyond it. He could no longer see the red-haired woman whose figure had so reminded him of that spectre whose terrible reality now seemed so difficult to believe: like a nightmare whose visceral terrors seem absurd in the glaring light of day.

"Yes," Mr Parker replied, "Mrs Astley of course, and a couple of her friends, and a gentleman from one of the local newspapers, I believe: you needn't speak to him unless you wish to, of course. Also Reverend Booth is expected from Thornedale – I don't know if you are acquainted with him. Perhaps his wife also? One or two others by the looks of it … and Reverend Vine of course, and his curate, ah there he is now … "

As they approached the small group standing a little way off from the open grave and the cheap wooden casket adorned with its simple wreath of flowers that rested close by the grave, Reverend Vine turned to greet them, his white clerical surplice billowing in the light breeze. Mr Corliss tried not to show his nervousness as the tall gentleman strode out to meet them, reaching out to shake their hands with a firm grasp. The carpenter dropped his gaze to the trailing white preaching bands that depending from the vicar's collar, unsure if he could look him in the eyes after what he done in the church. He felt so afraid that the reverend might see in his face the guilt he felt for violating the church as he had done. But their was something in the clergyman's easy smile, as he peered at them over his round spectacles, that told Mr Corliss he had no need to fear. Reverend Vine, at his ease, seemed utterly untroubled by any such suspicions.

"It's Mr Corliss, isn't it?" Reverend Vine's sonorous voice enquired as he gripped Mr Corliss' tender hand.

"Aye, aye it is, Reverend," Mr Corliss attempted to smile.

"Well, I am most gratified that you could come today. Shall we begin then, gentlemen?" Reverend Vine smoothed down his dark Imperial moustaches and goatee and adjusted his black clerical stole.

Mr Parker nodded eagerly and Reverend Vine turned, collecting himself in sober reflection as he strode solemnly around the casket and took his place at the head of the grave, his calm but serious countenance drawing the assembled group towards him.

Reverend Vine looked down towards the casket for a moment, took a deep breath and began.

"Man, that is born of a woman, hath but a short time to live, and is full of misery. He cometh up, and is cut down, like a flower; he fleeth as it were a shadow ... "

Mr Corliss half-expected that at any minute some accusing hand would fall upon his shoulder and denounce his body-stealing and his desecration of the church, and it took him some few minutes to calm his nerves and begin to feel a little easier. He looked around and reassured himself that there were no waiting policemen ready to detain him. Perhaps he had got away with it after all? He had taken such care to do right by Eliza and to cover his own tracks. Now in the daylight it occurred to him that the very strangeness of his acts might be protection enough: for who would ever even imagine that such a thing might have occurred? Two days had gone by and no-one had noticed anything amiss. Perhaps they never would?

All the while, as Reverend Vine continued his oration, another thought was gaining prominence in Mr Corliss' mind. He moved in a little closer, not wishing to see the grave, or the casket that he knew to be empty – save for the bag of rags and wood he had placed there – but to try to see more clearly the red-haired woman who had thus far been obscured from his view.

"O holy and most merciful Saviour, deliver us not into the bitter pains of eternal death. Thou knowest, Lord, the secrets of our hearts … "

Reverend Booth stood a few people away, his imposing height and broad chest obscuring the small-framed woman who stood on his far side, closer to the head of the grave. It was not Mrs Booth, whom he recognised, for she was a good deal taller, and Mr Corliss could plainly see her as she stood by another woman to his right. If Mr Corliss craned his head forward he could just make out the profile of this redheaded woman's lower face beneath the broad brim of her black hat. He shuddered and leaned back, his eyes searching again past Reverend Booth to try to see more of the woman. From the back he noticed only one detail: a stray tress of hair that trailed down over the collar and down the back of her simple black jacket. It was a most striking shade of red, threaded with one silver hair that caught the light. The hair curled prettily and a rising breath of wind caused it to wave in such a way that made Mr Corliss catch his breath. He tried not to look any more. He fixed his eyes on Reverend Vine, wondering, as he watched the vicar's white surplice undulating in the breeze, whether his prayers would help Eliza: whether God could forgive either her or Sir Benjamin for their wrongs, or whether He had simply forgotten them and their sins long ago.

"O merciful God, the Father of our Lord Jesus Christ, who is the resurrection and the life; in whom whosoever believeth, shall live, though he die; and whosoever liveth, and believeth in him, shall not die eternally …"

Mr Corliss closed his eyes tightly, praying in his thoughts not to God but to Eliza, lying buried in the church not far distant behind him: "*You have what you wanted now, Miss Eliza. I pray you find peace at last. I pray you go to your rest and walk this earth no more. Be at peace at last … and don't let them ever discover what I did for you …* "

"We humbly beseech thee, O Father, to raise us from the death of sin unto the life of righteousness … "

Mr Corliss raised his eyes to the pale grey skies above with a quiet sigh. His gaze wandered towards Mrs Astley, decked out in her finery, the black ostrich feathers ornamenting her large hat fluttered in the air. Standing some way behind her the newspaper reporter was quietly scribbling in his notebook. Mr Corliss' glance drifted down towards the grave, his brow wrinkling. "*And when my time comes, all these secrets will be buried with me. Who will ever know or care? Who will stand by my grave or remember me? What will I leave behind save for some shelves or a staircase? Perhaps this one deed is the best I can do. I could not help my mother but I could help Eliza. I hope that counts for something in the end — even if no-one else can ever know of it.*"

"Come, ye blessed children of my Father, receive the kingdom prepared for you from the beginning of the world. Grant this, we beseech thee, O merciful Father, through Jesus Christ, our Mediator and Redeemer. Amen. The grace of our Lord Jesus Christ, and the love of God, and the fellowship of the Holy Ghost, be with us all evermore. Amen."

As the little congregation dispersed and Mrs Astley drew Reverend Vine away to talk to the waiting reporter, Mr Corliss lingered, a few steps back from the grave, and a few feet away from Reverend Booth and the mysterious lady at his side as they remained by the graveside. Mr Corliss craned his neck to hear as Reverend Booth whispered quietly to the lady.

"There you see," Reverend Booth gestured discreetly towards Mrs Astley and the reporter, "it is the rich who write history once again … But fear not, the Lord knows all of his children and He knows, just as you and I know, who is buried here today. Even if no stone is placed, no name inscribed, we know it and He knows it: just as He knows the truth of what happened here all those years ago."

The lady in the hat merely nodded. Something caught in Mr Corliss' throat and he was mortified to hear himself cough, just once, but enough to make Reverend Booth turn around.

"Ah, it's Mr Corliss, is it not? I am very glad to see you – and looking so much better than when last we met, I am pleased to observe." Reverend Booth took a step back to reveal at last the lady at his side. Mr Corliss swallowed, trying to breathe as the blood drained from his head.

"I have someone here who was very desirous to meet you, Mr Corliss. May I introduce Mrs Ellis of whom I told you when you came to see me about … this matter."

Mr Corliss could only take off his hat and nod as the woman smiled and bowed her head a little to him. Beneath the large brim of her plain black hat, her face had all the shape and proportion of the spectre that had haunted him. Only to see at last the likeness of this face aglow with life and health; to see it smiling warmly; to see sparkling blue eyes shining out so warmly from such a face, nearly brought tears of wonder and joy to his eyes

... Mr Corliss thought for an instant: *"Yes, this is just how Eliza must have looked in all her beauty. Something of the goodness in her lives on here. She is so much alike, yet somehow so different."* There was a maturity in the woman's face that Eliza had never lived to achieve. There was a softness to her countenance so completely at odds with the fierceness he had come to associate with Eliza. Mrs Ellis' eyes were very kind and serene.

"H-how ... How do?" Mr Corliss managed at last.

"Oh, Mr Corliss," Mrs Ellis began in a soft voice, "I wanted to thank you for what you have done. It means such a great deal to me."

Reverend Booth looked around, as if concerned about who might hear. "I am wary of saying too much in this company, Mr Corliss, but I am very glad that the three of us can stand here today as witnesses to this burial, and as witnesses to the truth of Mistress Eliza's fate, as you have revealed it. Perhaps we, as her only true friends present here today, might each throw a handful of earth onto the casket – would you like that, Mrs Ellis?"

Mrs Ellis readily assented and rounded the grave where the excavated earth lay in a low dark mound. As the two men stood on the other side of the grave, Reverend Booth whispered to Mr Corliss.

"I should like to take this opportunity to invite you to my Sunday fellowship, Mr Corliss, if you would care to join us some time. In the afternoons, on Sundays, I open my home for a sociable gathering of friends. There is tea, interesting conversation, often a game of cards or some other amusement. You will always be made most welcome."

"Thank you, Reverend ... right good of you." Mr Corliss blinked, at a loss for words at the Reverend's generosity, and at the sudden desire he felt to be a part of such a fellowship.

As Mrs Ellis returned, Reverend Booth urged Mr Corliss to take his turn, and the carpenter trudged forwards, still smarting at all the aches in his body as he leaned down to collect a handful of earth. He thought of Eliza, in the church he could now see over Reverend Booth and Mrs Ellis' shoulders, and let the cool, damp earth fall from his hand into the grave, feeling some heavy weight fall from him as he let it go. He let out a deep sigh of relief.

As he began to walk back towards Reverend Booth and Mrs Ellis, his attention was caught by voices and movement to his right, and he turned to see the smiling face of Mr Parker beckoning him over to where the reporter and Mrs Astley now stood, waiting expectantly.

In the minute or two that it took to politely extricate himself from the reporter's requests that he might answer some questions about the discovery he had made at Wakeley Hall, Mr Corliss was a little dismayed to find that Reverend Booth and Mrs Ellis had joined Mrs Booth and some others in conversation in the churchyard a little way off from the grave. He hesitated, watching their backs as they chatted easily with Mrs Booth, the curate, and some other people whom Mr Corliss did not know.

Feeling still very tired – relieved that it was now all over and that that matter had apparently been laid to rest without his deeds being discovered – Mr Corliss crept quietly back around the side of the church and across the road to where Peggy stood sleepily waiting for him beneath the tall tree.

Mr Corliss dozed in his armchair by the fireplace, his hot cup of tea beginning to cool on the little table to his side and his copy of *Kipps* still waiting there to be finished. A quiet knocking at the door made him stir. He awoke with a start, his eyes frantically searching the room until he saw that he was quite alone. He put his hand on his chest and sighed as his body untensed. The knocking sounded again and Mr Corliss rubbed at his eyes and rose from the chair with a little groan, not quite sure what time it was or who might be at his door.

As he opened his front door his breath caught and he tried to cover his startled sound by clearing his throat. Mrs Ellis stood on his doorstep, the afternoon light behind her catching the coppery shine of her hair like a halo. Her kind face looked up into his.

"Hello again, Mr Corliss," she began. "Forgive me for disturbing you – were you asleep?"

"Ah, nay, it doesn't matter," Mr Corliss prevaricated, adjusting his neckcloth against the colour he felt rising in his skin.

"Reverend Booth told me you had been rather unwell recently."

"Ah, it was nowt but a cough," he forced a smile, noticing, over Mrs Ellis' shoulder, that Reverend and Mrs Booth were waiting in their carriage a little distance up the road: their backs to him as they conversed animatedly with each other.

"Only I had wanted to say back at the church," she faltered, her eyes crinkling as she struggled to express her thoughts, "I … I had wanted to thank you properly for finding Eliza, and for what you told Reverend Booth about the hairpin and all, you see … it proves the story that has been told by my family for generations: the story that no-one else believed about what kind of a terrible man that Sir Benjamin really was – least of all here in Wakeley … oh Mr Corliss, I'm sorry, I've upset you!"

Mr Corliss felt the warmth of Mrs Ellis' hand on his shoulder as his body shook with tears. Somehow he was suddenly weeping: it had just come over him before he even knew. His hands covered his face and he had instinctively turned away from her.

"Here," her gentle voice soothed as she put her slender around him and guided him inside the house and back to his armchair by the fire. He couldn't speak for some moments as his tears flowed and he fumbled for his handkerchief. Mrs Ellis said nothing, but simply sat near him, quietly, her eyes filled with tender sympathy.

"My father killed my mother you see," he heard himself saying at last. "I was told never to speak of it either. Never to tell anyone. My grandparents took me in – they said it would only bring shame on us if anyone ever knew. I've never told anyone since then until today. I … I don't know why but I thought you would understand somehow … " He searched her eyes and saw that they were moist with sympathetic tears. She nodded her head.

"Yes, I know what it is to be burdened by a secret, Mr Corliss, and I know the pain of bereavement, although I cannot pretend to know the suffering of a child robbed of his mother so very cruelly."

"Miss Eliza, she touched me," he struggled to explain. "Knowing what that man did to her, I … I …" he trailed off.

Mrs Ellis leaned forward and lightly touched Mr Corliss' hand, her small fingers resting over his, covering the missing tip of his finger. "Perhaps she was waiting for such a kind man as you. Perhaps she knew that you would understand and that you would see that truth of it."

Mr Corliss did not know what to say and merely tried to smile, wiping at his face with his handkerchief and drawing in a deep breath as Mrs Ellis leaned back in her chair.

"Forgive me," he said, his eyes staring down into the coals of the fire, suddenly feeling keen embarrassment at his loss of composure.

"There is nothing to forgive, Mr Corliss. I am glad I could bear witness for you and your mother, just as you have borne witness to Miss Eliza. I can see that you are very tired and still recovering from your illness. I will leave you to your rest."

She stood up, straightening her long black skirt and stepping onto the rug, turning back to face Mr Corliss. Mr Corliss' eyes widened to see her standing there upon the very spot where Eliza's shade had stood.

"Reverend Booth said that we might perhaps see you at one of his fellowship meetings?"

"Oh aye, perhaps I will come." He stood up.

"I do hope so."

Mr Corliss saw Mrs Ellis to the door and watched as she walked off up the drive to the waiting carriage, waving as she turned back. Reverend Booth turned back to wave also as Mrs Ellis settled herself in the carriage.

"Goodbye then, Mr Corliss, and don't forget, any Sunday after three. We shall be expecting you … "

Mr Corliss awoke early on Monday morning after sleeping most of the weekend, and decided that he was well enough to return to his work at Wakeley Hall.

It was with some trepidation that he walked back into the cavernous cellars, and switched on the electric lights. But somehow the air seemed clearer, as if the stale, unwholesome odour had at last drifted away. He carried in his toolbox and set it down, hearing his steps echoing through the vaulted chambers but feeling no fear as he approached the section of the wall that had broken under his pressure only a week before. The wall had been repaired and little evidence now remained to show where anything untoward had happened, save for the lighter colour of the new mortar where the wall had been rebuilt.

Mr Corliss ran his hand over the cool bricks in the wall and let out a deep sigh. The mortar had set and dried. The wall was solid and strong again. He nodded his head to himself, deciding that he would install the shelves in that section, as he had intended to do when the wall had broken open. His head tilted at the suggestion of a sound echoing in the cellar and he spun around, relieved to see that it was only Mr Parker entering the cellars, waving at him as he walked briskly through the first cellar and into the second.

"How are we feeling today, Mr Corliss? I must say you look much recovered."

"Fine, sir, thank you." Mr Corliss could still hear the hoarseness in his voice, but it was improving each day.

"Grand, that's grand. I am very pleased to hear it. I must say I was rather worried about that cough of yours last week. I was afraid that the bad air down here had really done you some harm. It seems much fresher down here though now, doesn't it? I expect what with Mr Langdale and his assistant, and all the other comings and goings in here over the past week or so have moved the air about a bit, stirred things up a bit, so that's good." He smiled and rubbed his hands together. "I just wanted to let you know that we seem to have sorted out all those problems we were having at the dairy last week so some of the men should be free to lend you a hand this afternoon, once they've finished unloading the new farm machinery that's arrived today."

"That's right good of you, Mr Parker."

"Not at all. It's good to have you back on deck, as it were."

Mr Corliss smiled and drew his pencil and measuring tape from his apron pocket, making ready to begin his work on the repaired section of wall.

"Yes," he heard Mr Parker take a few steps away behind him, and the familiar sound of Mr Parker rubbing his hands together, "yes, quite a different atmosphere all together down here now. Remarkable. Splendid, in fact."

He heard Mr Parker's footsteps hesitate.

"You'll probably think me quite ridiculous, Mr Corliss. Mr Astley has often ridiculed me on this subject, but over the years of working at Wakeley Hall I have been aware of certain ... peculiar atmospheres ... ah, certain odd things that happen at the Hall ... "

Mr Corliss' hair prickled and he turned to face Mr Parker, trying not to appear as intensely desirous to hear more as he felt. "Odd things, sir … ?"

Mr Parker smiled a sort of embarrassed smile and looked slightly sheepish. Mr Corliss was surprised to see Mr Parker's confidence falter, and felt somehow reassured by it. "Ah, yes – perhaps you've heard some of the other fellows talking about such things? The ghost stories associated with the Hall and so on?" he asked hopefully.

"Well, yes, as a matter of fact." Mr Corliss swallowed, worried that his eyes were open too wide. "I have heard things … "

"Well, it's the most curious thing," Mr Parker explained nervously, scratching his sandy hair in exasperation. "I know some people think it quite ridiculous, but, well, just as many of the staff here have, I have always heard the coughing – the phantom coughing, as it were – why it's become so commonplace to me over the years I've just grown used to it I suppose. Well, I didn't like to say anything to you, but I even heard it that first day we came down here into the cellars together. I was frankly glad you didn't hear it, as it has scared off some staff over the years, believe it or not. But that seems happily beside the point now. The odd thing is that it seems to have stopped altogether. No-one has heard the cough since the wall … was opened. That peculiar atmosphere I so often felt – particularly down here – why it's simply … gone … " Mr Parker raised his sandy eyebrows in puzzlement. He searched Mr Corliss' face for some reaction, fearful of the ridicule he had so often encountered before when the subject had come up.

"Well, I … " Mr Corliss struggled for words, "I do believe in such things, as it happens."

Mr Parker nodded with evident relief. "I can't help but wonder, Mr Corliss, if, by your discovery, you have allowed that unhappy soul to find its rest at last? Perhaps it was not Lady Stockard's shade at all that has haunted Wakeley Hall these many years, but rather … " Mr Parker gestured towards the newly bricked up wall, " … she … "

"Eliza," Mr Corliss stated quietly, unravelling his measuring tape and placing his pencil behind his ear. "Eliza Burns."

"I was almost going to mention it to you the other night when I came to your house but you seemed so very ill and I didn't want to worry you – in fact, I rather thought that I had imagined hearing that same phantom cough on that occasion."

"The other night?"

"Yes, when I came to see how you were and you had that terrible fit of coughing in your parlour, well – it sounds so ridiculous to say it – but I fancied that I heard the coughing then, in your house of all places. No, I'm sure it was just an echo from the fireplace or something. I suppose the discovery of the body had me a bit spooked, as it did all of us here. Well, all except Mr Astley whose nerves are made of far sterner stuff." Mr Parker smiled. "In any case, I'm very glad that you have recovered so well from your illness, Mr Corliss, and I look forward to seeing more shelves going up this week. Do let me know if you need anything, won't you?"

"A-Aye, I-I will, Sir."

"Cheerio, then."

Mr Corliss stood staring at the wall as Mr Parker's footsteps echoed away and out of the cellars. He measured and marked the spot where he had tried to drill before. Picking up his brace and bit he positioned the point of the drill on his mark and leaned his weight against the smooth wooden head of the brace. It did not yield. It did not give way. Mr Corliss smiled and began to turn the handle.

***

ACKNOWLEDGEMENTS

I would like to thank Steve Letford, Erin D Vine, Dan Vine, Christopher Hamerton, Stephen Mosley, Richard May, Stephen Bates and Roy Barry for their kind and generous help with researching various aspects of this story.

ABOUT THE AUTHOR

TANIA DONALD is a Melbourne-based author and artist. Her first novel, HAUNTED HEART was published by Penguin in 2011. She holds a Ph.D in English Literature and has written for theatre, radio and cabaret. She is also the author of THE BOOK OF CALLING, the forthcoming novel DEAD MAN'S FINGERS, and two other novellas, THE HAEMOPHILIAC and THE WRECK OF THE CONTESSA ELISABETTA.

Tania is inspired by classic literature of the fantastic, with favourite authors including H. P. Lovecraft and M. R. James. She is also an admirer of classic horror films, particularly Universal Horror and the films of Hammer.

www.ingramcontent.com/pod-product-compliance
Lightning Source LLC
Chambersburg PA
CBHW021927170626
46807CB00007B/3013